Yoo Pee Funny

A Comic's Eye-view of the U.P.

by

DALE R. HOFFMAN

This novel is a work of fiction. Names, characters, places, and incidents are either the product of the author's imagination or are used fictitiously and any resemblance to actual persons, businesses, events, is coincidental.

http://www.drumcomic.com
http://www.northwoodscomedy.com

Deerwood Books

Cover design by
Rob S. Furr
http://furr.ca/

Cover Photographs by
April Hoffman

Library of Congress Control Number: 2012933523

ISBN: 0-9835125-4-X
ISBN-13: 978-0-9835125-4-7

Dedication

For all of the Yoopers who work way too hard for not enough money. In life, we sing the same songs and laugh at the same jokes. In death, maybe we'll own our own mining company.

Forward

People buy books for something to read. This book hasn't even started yet and here you are reading already.

Backward

I was going to write a *real* forward for this book but in retrospect, my life has been nothing but backwards. As a comic, I spent years beating out jokes in comedy clubs and still do. For all of my efforts I have been rewarded with a life of hard work and obscurity, but then no one is ever guaranteed success in anything, least of all show business.

I want you to know that comedy is what I live for. We're all going to die some day so we may as well die laughing. I feel I have had a successful career, as long as money isn't the meter for which my success is measured.

Comedy led me to my wife and a beautiful farm in a place called The Upper Peninsula of Michigan. Without comedy, these things would still be unknown to me. I'm the writing type of comic and that has freed my soul as well as anything else.

You see there are two types of comics—the acting type and the writing type. If you want to succeed in comedy you need to learn to do both, but some comics are just natural actors while others are just natural writers. Sometimes the writers have trouble on stage selling their own material and sometimes the actors have trouble using material that belongs to them.

The writers can have crooked faces, bad teeth, and are not so popular within the industry. The actors can be wildly popular within the industry and go on to achieve some type of great financial success or are simply never heard from again.

The writing type of comics can have long, unusual careers, bounce from one gig to the next and then when they're sixty and out of work, they check into a Hollywood hotel and drink a bottle of antifreeze mixed with Gatorade.

Fortunately for me, I already wasted four years of my life in Hollywood. Even if I did go back to visit, I never really cared for Gatorade in the first place. Besides, I have a great wife and family and that's reason enough not to go.

The Upper Peninsula (U.P.) has been nothing but great to me. I think this is true because I'm so weird and the U.P. tends to welcome weirdness with open arms. In any event, my farm is working out, there are outlets for comedy and I have a full four seasons that provide a completely different landscape every three months, which is perfect for the restless spirit.

Spring really springs, summer swelters and cools, fall falls quickly and winter hits like a ton of bricks. The outdoor adventures are limitless and so are the treasured premises that comics covet. If I didn't think Yoopers had a good sense of humor I wouldn't have written this book—but they do—so here it is.

CHAPTER I. BACK NORTH

I grew up in the industrial north about thirty miles outside of Pittsburgh. In the eighties, my family left the area for a better economic situation in the Southeast, along with everyone else from Western PA.

In fact, for a while, Detroit and Pittsburgh had the same slogan, "Last one out shut off the lights." Twenty-some years later I find myself here in the U.P., in a climate I swore I would never tolerate again. But I have to say that it is a blast.

One of my favorite things about living back north is remembering all the things I used to know when I was younger, but have since forgotten. For example, free refrigeration. I totally forgot about that one. Cold beer outside, warm fire inside, that's the recipe for a great winter.

Socks and winter boots—I forgot all about how a pair of rubber boots will pull down one of your socks. Then you have a choice— do I take my boot off and pull my sock up or do I just let it fall off my foot and walk around in boots with one bare foot? Now, three U.P. winters later, I always make sure that when I work outside, I'm wearing some long socks with good elastic.

Generally up north, socks are very important. When I lived in North Carolina I went about six straight years without ever putting on a pair of socks. One year, I don't even think I wore underwear. What a year.

The wood stove—now there's a flashback. Right now I have a temperature gauge on my woodstove that lets me know if it's over-firing, and yes, I over fired it the first spring I owned it. When I was a teenager, like a lot of other Pennsylvania families, I lived in a house that was built into the side of a hill. This design created a massive basement that became my bedroom when my sister left for college, woodstove included.

That stove was piped through the wall, not the ceiling, and I remember cramming that thing full of wood with *no* temperature gauge while my high school buddies and I caught a buzz and listened to "Slow Ride," the longest song ever. Amazingly enough, the house is still standing and here I am today. So either they made better woodstoves back then or the current gauge on my woodstove is crap.

The price of cigarettes—fortunately, I quit over five years ago and thank God. Forget the health aspects—seven bucks a pack? I used to live twenty miles from the RJ Reynolds plant and a *carton* was fifteen bucks. I remember when I moved to Los Angeles, I couldn't believe I was paying four bucks a pack, now it's seven? One thing is for sure, as long as I live in Michigan, I'll never start smoking again.

Frozen mud—I forgot what it felt like to walk around in the pure slop of semi-frozen mud and slush. In the spring on my farm I'm like one of the peasants in Monty Python's Holy Grail, groveling around in the cold mud complaining about the repression of the broken political system. "You're the king? Well I didn't vote for you! Do you see him repressing me?"

Something else I love about the North—few snakes. For fifteen years I lived in Wilmington North Carolina, a fun town and my Alma-mater, but host to more varieties of poisonous snakes than anywhere in the U.S. In fact, Wilmington is the northernmost subtropical point in the U.S, so they get the temperate poisonous snakes *and* the southern ones, gators too—big ones.

The also have creepy spiders. I can deal with the wolf spiders up here even though they bite, carpenter ants, too, but at least they don't kill you when they bite you. Yeah, yeah brown recluse—let me tell you something—in the South, forget the black widows and brown recluses, they have poisonous spiders that will kill you that most people have never even *heard of*. You'll just be sick and not know why.

But that doesn't matter because you're much more likely to die from standing on a hill of fire ants. My friend stood on a hill once and ended up in the emergency room with his head swollen up like The Great Pumpkin. "Holy ant hills, you're going to die, Charlie Brown!" They gave him a shot just in time to save his life.

People complain about the flies up here, but at least they don't bite. The black flies are bad, but they're only bad certain times of the year. In the South, the houseflies bite—like a freakin' mosquito! They have little shiny green heads and you don't feel them land, like a horsefly or deerfly, and it's year-round.

They have these jumping spiders, too. They're like a cross between a grasshopper and a spider, not poisonous, but they jump like six feet in the air, all up in your face—a jumping spider for crying out loud! Aren't the crawling ones enough?

Flying cockroaches too—they call them Japanese water bugs. You see, people are polite in the South. No matter where you go, everyone has a different name for the cockroaches in that vicinity, but it's never called a cockroach! "Oh that's a water bug", or, "It's a Palmetto bug," or "It's a Japanese water bug."

"Japanese water bug? That's a flying cockroach and it's freaky, man!"

I do miss surfing warm water. You can't beat sitting on a surfboard in eighty-degree water on an eighty-five degree day, but I'm middle-aged now anyway and I'd probably need Viagra to get up on a surfboard. People used to say, "Aren't you afraid of sharks when you surf?"

I'd say, "Sharks? Have you seen the *bugs* around here? How do you sleep at night?"

I'll say this about the water in the North—icy cold, crystal-clean, well water. I can drink gallons of it. Some of my friends have wells in NC and the water comes out lukewarm! Gross! So, I guess it's a trade off. I gave up the warm *swimming* water for cold *drinking* water.

I broke even on a lot of other things, too—traded ocean fish for lake fish—also broke even on the accent. I gave up Southern accents for Yooper accents. You know what's funny? Either place you can use all of the same jokes. Everyone knows who Hank and Willie are.

One of the best things about the U.P. is the light traffic. Sure, it's a long drive to get to where you're going, but what a great drive, even in the worst winter weather it's still just a beautiful drive. After twenty years of attempting to navigate gridlock—what a drive! I'm actually driving, not sitting. I love it! I'm the guy that lets everyone pass him.

I once heard a woman complain about the cold. I said, "It's the U.P. Why do you live here if you don't like the cold?"

She said, "I can't afford to move."

We were in a casino. You see the point I'm making here?

Yoopers aren't afraid to have a party either, and they don't even need a good reason. I found this to be especially true throughout the course of a year spent living in the Houghton/Hancock area. The Keweenaw has a festival for all occasions from Winter Carnival to Heikenpäivähh(sp?) to my favorite party of all—Bridge-fest. That's really pushing the boundaries of alcoholism there, "Look it's a bridge ... let's get drunk!"

(Insert the sound of twist-off caps)

Any town that gets drunk because there's a bridge, is a town that likes to party.

"What other inanimate objects can we drink to?" Hey it's a chair—Chair-fest! Look it's a sign—Sign-fest!"

"Did it snow today?"

"Sure did."

"Snow-fest!"

"I have to go to the dentist."

"Bridgework-fest!"

And the worse the weather gets, the bigger the party they throw. In January, they line up to take a polar bear jump in the canal, into a hole in the ice that the firemen cut open *for* them. Naturally, there are plenty of paramedics and rescue people on hand. I mean, I've been to some keg parties before and I've seen people end up in the emergency room once or twice, but I've never had the paramedics actually standing by ... waiting. Now that's a party!

So what the heck, I guess I'll stay. I have twenty acres and all the free firewood I can burn.

I'll spend my days walking around in my one-sock boots over-firing my woodstove, drinking clean cold water and thanking God that the houseflies don't bite. Maybe I'll have a little party on my back twenty.

"Acre-fest!"

* *Back North* first appeared in *U.P. Magazine, from* Porcupine Press Publications.

CHAPTER II. WELCOME WHOMEVER

You see the signs every year on the hotels, bars and restaurants around the U.P. The signs change with the seasons: "Welcome Fishermen, Welcome Hunters, Welcome Snowmobilers," and my all time favorite—"Welcome Bikers."

Think about this. It's summer and the bikers are coming. Whether you *want* the bikers or not, you *better* put up a sign that says—"Welcome Bikers." Does anyone *not* welcome the bikers? I'd like to see the guy with *this* sign, "Kiss my chops, bikers. I shot Snake and stole his crystal-meth." That's bound to be a popular establishment during the summer months. "Local restaurant burned to cinders, details at eleven."

A friend of mine said, "No dude, the bikers these days aren't like the gang type of bikers they had in the old days. They're just the snowmobilers in the summer time. It's a bunch of dentists and business owners."

Dentists and business owners? What do they call themselves, Hell's Chamber of Commerce?

I've been thinking about who else we can welcome and how else we can welcome them. There are so many different groups of tourists that visit the U.P. Maybe we should start combining them into made-up words on one big sign, give the tourists something to talk about.

For example, instead of separate signs that say, "Welcome Bikers, Welcome Fishermen Welcome Campers, Welcome Hikers, Welcome ATVers," we could just have a sign that says, "Welcome Fimpker-V'ers."

I can hear the tourists now, "Welcome Fimpker-V'ers? Must be Finnish."

This one combines Snowmobilers, Skiers, Snowshoers, Hunters, and Ice Fisherman: Welcome Skowshuntermen!" The Japanese tourists will never figure that one out—sounds like Godzilla. "Run! The Skowshuntermen are coming!"

The summertime is an especially eclectic mix of people in the U.P. This one combines car clubbers, loggers and hippies. "Welcome Cloggies!" We could even dress that one up with a nice picture of a tricked-out log picker painted in flower power. Peace, car shows and toilet paper, that kind of thing.

The U.P. is an original, one-of-a-kind place. We should have some welcome signs just for each other. "Welcome Yoopers! You know who you are! Enjoy your stay!" I think that might build morale.

I had another idea, too. Maybe we should see how much we could get away with. For example, we could welcome certain groups of people, but kind of insult them at the same time.

"Welcome Snowmobilers! Bring your gasoline smelling asses on in!" or "Welcome Fisherman! We don't care *how* much your fingers stink!" or, "Welcome Car Clubbers! Forget about those trophy bucks you ran over on the way here!" I suppose if I owned a local business I'd probably go with a more conservative approach.

Another thought occurred to me about this whole welcoming thing. I don't see too many goodbye signs. Wouldn't it be fun to put some of those on the Wisconsin state line? "Later Bikers. Don't let the door hit you where The Lord split you." or "Hey hunters, peace out!" "Hey ATVers—our mud is now your mud." Here's a couple for the color-tour people. "See, they were just leaves." Or "You're now leafing the U.P." (Groan)

So the conclusion one must draw from this nonsense is that it's impossible to target every group simultaneously. So why even try? I propose we just keep it nice and general. I propose only one sign. "Welcome Whomever With Whatever!" That could be the foundation for the new U.P. travel campaign. "Welcome whomever with whatever. You're welcome to do whichever, wherever and whenever."

People will travel from miles away. We'll ask them why they came and they'll say, "I just came to do whichever, wherever and whenever, and to feel welcome doing whatever."

"Hello, bureau of tourism?"

It's not unusual for people to go overboard when welcoming others. I'm not sure if this is still true, but West Virginia's state slogan used to be, "West Virginia—Open for Business."

Well I should hope so. It could be discouraging for Interstate travelers if the sign read, "West Virginia—Closed 'Til Mornin'" or "West Virginia will be closed Monday, February 15 for President's Day. Drive Safely."

That's another one that drives me nuts, "Drive Safely." It seems like states are always lumping that one in with their own sign. "Welcome to Kansas—The Pancake State—Drive Safely."

Does anyone drive safely because of that sign? People are too used to ignoring safety warnings to even come *close* to following a sign like that. If you want people to drive safely you need to get their attention. Build a sign with a people icon and a jackass icon and an arrow pointing to the jackass. "Don't be this." That's a sign people will remember. Of course, half the people out there would say to themselves, "Wow, they must hate the Democrats."

Right now on the Pure Michigan website the pitch is, "A better state—the state of Michigan." That's nice.

We should have a Pure Yooper website. "A drunker peninsula—the Upper Peninsula. Bring cash because we don't take a debit card."

So enjoy your summer, wave at the bikers and hikers and cyclists and campers and R.V. people; wave at all the swimmers and church groups and ATVers and fishermen, and when you see them go by, say to yourself: "Welcome, whomever with whatever." And when you have a chance to talk to those people, ask them if they did whichever wherever and whenever. I doubt they'll disagree.

* *Welcome Whomever* first appeared in Porcupine Press Publications *U.P. Magazine, vol 21 #6.*

CHAPTER III. DRIVING THE DOG FOR A WALK

One of the most interesting phenomenons I've noticed in the U.P. is that of driving the dog for a walk. This is where a person drives their car down a country road while the dog runs along the side of the road. If oncoming traffic approaches, the person stops the car and calls the dog. The dog jumps in the car and when oncoming traffic passes, the person lets the dog back out of the car to run down the side of the road again while they drive.

I first noticed this last winter. I was shoveling snow and a blue car came bumping along my country road and I realized that the person was driving their dog for a walk. I thought to myself, well that's a good idea. *It's freezing out here. Why not sit inside a toasty warm car while the dog exercises at his own expense? Iditarod be damned!*

Summer. It was seventy-five degrees outside and not only was the blue car still driving *their* dog for a walk but two or three other cars were now driving *their* dogs for a walk as well. Now I think to myself, "Is there a parade I don't know about? *Will there be fire trucks and a marching band? What other types of animals do they drive out here? Maybe a tractor will come by with a pig running along side? Maybe it's a club? Maybe it's a scheduled event?"*

"Welcome once again to dog-drivers of the western U.P. Today we'll be driving a Cock-a-poo, a Maltese terrier and four Beagles down Union Avenue. Tell the dogs to take a right at the post office then head west until noon. We'll meet for lunch at Pet-smart."

I've walked my dog plenty. I've driven my dog plenty. I've never done both at the same time. It kind of reminds me of the old out-of-shape phys-ed teacher who rides in a golf-cart beside his students while they run cross-country.

The laziest person I ever met was a guy from college. He liked to watch football and drink beer, but he didn't want to get off the couch, so instead of making trips to the bathroom he used empty two-liter bottles. He brought a whole new meaning to the phrase *hanging out on football night*.

I said, "Man, every time we come over here you have two-liter Pepsi bottles next to your couch full of pee. At least use Mountain Dew bottles so it doesn't look so disgusting."

I don't know what happened to that guy but I doubt he's hosting too many Super Bowl Parties.

I wouldn't place dog-drivers in the category of lazy. I'd classify them as lazy but interesting. Who knows, maybe it's a growth industry? Someone should invent a leash that attaches directly to the front bumper of the car. Maybe we could program an automatic retractable leash into an On-star system. "Approaching traffic—now reeling in the dog—repeat—now reeling in the dog."

Something else occurred to me. What is the dog thinking? If you say to the dog, *do you want to go for a walk*—does he run to the car? Can you imagine this dog talking to regular sled dogs? "Wait a minute, you mean you guys have to *pull?*"

I suppose if a squirrel can water-ski a dog will be happy to be driven for a walk. There have been dancing bears, high diving horses and let's not forget the multi-tasking monkeys. Oh, the monkeys.

In Britain, a man lost his license for six months after driving *his* dog for a stroll. Paul Railton was spotted by a cyclist driving slowly along a country lane, holding his dog's leash through the car window. Naturally, the anal-retentive cyclist called the fuzz.

Hey @$$hole, either join the police force or ride a mountain bike!

Paul pled guilty to the charge, but told the court: *A lot of people exercise their dogs in that manner. You should check out the U.P. of Michigan!*

His lawyer stated that Mr. Railton doesn't normally drive in such a manner, but added: "It was a silly thing to do and there was an element of laziness."

Dumbass! Don't people in England know how to pretend they're handicapped? I see people doing that all the time in this country! Mr. Railton was ordered to pay a £66 fine. What is that, Monopoly money? Also, they added three points to his driver's license, which means absolutely nothing in a country so small you could probably hike the entire perimeter in two weeks.

At least the guy only had one pet. Some people have too many pets—four dogs, eight cats, a turtle, ferret, fish, iguana, cockatiel-bird that never shuts up, hamsters, gerbils, a sixteen-foot python in the back room and of course, mice and rats to feed the python. I had a neighbor like that once. Every time you stopped by, there was always a giant pile of poop on the living room floor.

I said, "Man you live in an apartment, what the heck are you doing with all of these pets?"

He said, "I just love animals. I'm like a zoo-keeper."

I said, "Yeah but zoo-keepers don't live *inside* the cage. You see the difference?"

For me, the only acceptable time to sleep near a bathroom area is after tequila-night. But I'll say this in my zookeeper neighbor's defense—at least he gets up to use the bathroom for himself. That's more than I can say for two-liter bottle guy and he didn't have *any* pets.

* *Driving the Dog for a Walk* first appeared in the Jan/Feb 2011 issue of *U.P. Magazine,* from Porcupine Press Publication.

CHAPTER IV. DISCOUNT ON ME

Everybody wants a discount these days. I just want my college years back. What a waste. I went to culinary school. Some people have a passion for cooking in a commercial kitchen. I do not. I have a passion for sitting at a table and eating a steak.

In retrospect, it was ludicrous for me to go to college for restaurant work. For some of us, the whole point of going to college is so we don't end up working in a restaurant for the rest of our lives. In fact, the very first day of culinary school the first thing my chef said to our class was, "You don't need to go to school to work in a restaurant.

You should already have a job in a restaurant right now."

And I did. And for some reason I continued to return to this institution on a daily basis.

Going to culinary school was perhaps the biggest waste of money in my life—five thousand dollars to make ten bucks an hour and at the end of the night I had to mop the floor and take out the trash. I wasn't a chef. I was a janitor who cooked. Who knows, maybe I'll go back to college and get a Masters Degree in mowing grass.

No one will ever tell you the truth about kitchen work either. They'll all tell you that cooking is an honorable profession. Honorable? I don't think so. What other profession can you have two shirtsleeves of tattoos and people still address you as sir. I'll tell you what an honorable profession is—Judge. That's why when people walk into a courtroom they say, "Excuse me, may I please speak, Your Honor?"

No one says that when they walk into a kitchen. You know what they say? "Where's my food *&%hole?"

"If you could just get me that chicken sandwich, that'd be great, Your Honor. If court is in session now I'll be taking a side of fries with that, too."

There are those, however, who simply love food and drink, and most of us have worked in a restaurant. I've always said that there are two kinds of people that work in a restaurant—highly trained professionals, and anyone else who showed up for the interview.

It's frustrating for professional restaurant people when incompetent people are hired, because we know that it's a life-or-death situation. Every year in the U.S., 100,000 people get sick from food poisoning and 5,000 of them die. That's right, 5,000 people go out to eat and never come home—or come home briefly. You should have to be a doctor to work in a restaurant. I'd like to hear that one on the intercom, "Doctor Johnson to salad prep, Doctor Johnson to salad prep—code green."

I've worked every position in a restaurant except Manager and that'll never happen because who wants to spend seventy hours a week at work? I'm a professional comic and I didn't even wwant to work seventy hours a week at *that* job.

I cook at home for my wife and that's enough cooking for me. Waiting tables part-time is much easier, but I can assure you, there are few things as depressing as waiting tables. People always want to talk down to you.

Here's what I love about waiting tables—the kitchen is 104 degrees, the dining room is a comfy 70. Here's what I hate about waiting tables—nametags. Nametags put you at an immediate disadvantage with a customer—they know your name and you don't know theirs. Sometimes they want to exploit that.

"Um, yeah, can I get some more bread—(look at my chest)—uh, Dale?"

"Sure. Do you want some butter for your bread—(look at crotch)—Dick?

In fact, people and their bread generally ticks me off. It's just bread, it's not the end of the world.

"Do you have whole-grain bread?"

"Rye do you ask? Wheat kind of bread would you like? We have whole-grain but we *barley* have any left."

That's whole-grain humor, just for the Midwest.

I waited tables at a casino for a while. That's a tough gig because half the people coming through the front door just lost on the tables and now they're either angry or they want something for free—or both. Generally these people feel the need to take out their frustrations on the service staff.

I greeted an old couple at the front door one time. I said, "Hi Guys."

She scowled at me and said, "Hi Guys yourself!"

I said, "Smoking or non-smoking," because what am I going to say, "Right this way, Loser?"

That's another frustrating thing about waiting tables instead of doing comedy shows. At a comedy show you can tell stupid people that they are in fact, stupid. You can illustrate it, spell it out, make light of it and rub it in ... deep. You can't do that to customers in a restaurant no matter how moronic they are.

And as far as angry gamblers go, I have no pity for people who lose in a casino. Learn how to control yourself. I don't care what kind of psychological disorder your shrink says you have. If you're willing to lose five hundred dollars on a craps table and can't even leave the waitress who brings your food a lousy five bucks, either you or your parents failed.

Everybody wants a discount these days, that's for sure. Every day someone is talking about how bad the economy is. "The economy is bad, the economy is bad." I'm a comedian; the economy has always sucked for me. Even in the late nineties when I was on tour, buying gas in Georgia for eighty cents a gallon, I still had to sell four t-shirts to get to the next show. In fact, when it comes to the U.S. economy, the U.P. is better off than a lot of places because it's kind of self-containing. Things grow, but also kind of stay the same.

The tourist economy in the U.P. is on the rise, but the toughest part of the tourist economy is that the off-season is five months a year—spring and fall. Even with the hunters in the fall it's not really that busy. So I'm here to help on this one. Maybe the "coupon people," those who print the money-saving paper tickets that Yoopers love so much, could implement some of these coupons for next year.

10 YOOPER COUPONS FOR THE OFF SEASON

(Good for October, November, March, April and May)

1. **"No Coupon-Coupon"**—Any Yooper who walks into any U.P. retail business, bar or restaurant with absolutely no coupons, tickets, vouchers, certificates, newspaper clippings, mailers, stipulations, grandfather clauses, pre-existing conditions, friend or family relations or any other method of obtaining a discount, and simply just spends

some money in that establishment, automatically receives two dollars off.

2. **The Recycler**—Pick up ten cans by the side of any U.P. road and automatically receive up to one dollar. (Michigan cans only.)

3. **The Beamer**—Twenty five cents off your next gallon of gas for anyone who just turns their high beams down instead of milking it to the very last possible second so that oncoming traffic doesn't have to flash you with their high beams to tell you to turn your beams down.

4. **The Slugger** — Five bucks off your next bar tab for not fist-fighting and just having fun while you're drunk. Only two dollars off if you don't fight, but whine about your ex-wife or girlfriend all night.

5. **The Tall Tale**—One dollar off your next box of ammo just for believing the "*I saw something unusually large or creepy out in the woods*" story that your buddy tells you. We've all seen something weird or amazing

things out there, yet none of us believe each other!

6. **The Body Shot**—Your first drink is free for anyone who puts on deodorant during the off-season before going out in public. We know work is slow, Dude. Do it for *us*—please.

7. **The Self-Amuser**—Ten percent off any sporting goods purchase at any U.P. retail store for any person who makes up a new winter sport during a spring or fall snowstorm, e.g., snow blower races, pulling sleds behind ATV's, snowman wrestling, drift-swimming, lying in beach loungers in the snow, pretending you're somewhere tropical, etc.

8. **The Opener**—Add ten percent to the bottom line of your business just for staying open. You own a gas station. It's Monday at two o'clock in the afternoon. Why are you closed?

9. **The Literate**—Fifteen percent off your next book or magazine purchase if you can

spell peninsula, maintenance and restaurant on the first try without reading this. Oops, too late.

10. **The *Go Humans** Coupon**—Free pat on the back for anyone who gives to charity, volunteers their time, or cares about something other than money—like other people—even the ones they don't know.

Use any or all of these coupons in conjunction with one or another at any time during either slow season. Together we can clip our way to another productive spring and fall in the U.P.

Discount on me , first appeared in the Nov/Dec 2010 issue of *U.P. Magazine,* from Porcupine Press.

****Go Humans*** t-shirt available online at:
http://www.drumcomic.com/store.html

CHAPTER V: THE RE-WIKIPE-DICULOUS HISTORY OF MICHIGAN

Thousands of years before the arrival of the first Europeans, several indigenous tribes lived in what is today the state of Michigan. They were members of the Algonquian family of Amerindians and this included a tribe called Miami. Did you say Miami? Snowbirds—another thing the white man took credit for!

The first European explorer to visit Michigan was the Frenchman Étienne Brûlé. In 1620, he began his expedition from Quebec City, on a mandate to find those responsible for the difficult pronunciation of his name. Upon reaching Michigan he abandoned this mission in search of soft cheese. He later died in Wisconsin of an overdose.

The French built several trading posts in what is now Detroit. The employees were immediately laid off. War broke out and it was during this period that the people of Detroit lost every single battle with the British, abroad as well as at home. The Lions were born.

The revolutionary war ended with the signing of the Treaty of Paris in 1783, and Michigan passed into the control of the newly formed United States of America. Everyone ate a big dinner and continued passing throughout the evening.

In 1787, the region became part of the Northwest Territory. The plan was to shoot a film starring Jimmy Stewart, but the British continued to occupy Detroit and Jimmy Stewart wasn't born yet. The British finally left the area in 1796, after the implementation of the Jay Treaty.

The Jay Treaty mandated that both sides smoke a doobie and forget the whole thing. Also, no more wars should be fought in wigs, ruffled shirts and double-breasted button-down coats. Said one statesman, "Reloading after each shot is one thing, but these clothes are ridiculous!" Years later, the battle would be re-enacted over and over again by lonely, middle-aged men who like to dress up in Tri-corns.

In 1800, Michigan became part of the Indiana Territory. Most of the land was declared as Michigan Territory in 1805, including all of the Lower Peninsula except, of course, for Indiana ... d'uh!

During the War of 1812, British forces from Canada captured Detroit and Fort Mackinac, but they just couldn't eat any more of that Mackinac fudge so they returned the fort a year later. "Forget it we're stuffed. Get this fudge away from us!"

Michigan's oldest university, the University of Michigan, was founded in Detroit in 1817, and was later moved to its present location in Ann Arbor. It's been called the single greatest feet of human strength in history, when the people of Detroit picked up the university and carried it all the way to Ann Arbor, placing it down ever so gently. Mayflower moving company was later founded.

Between 1870 and 1890, the population of Michigan doubled. Almost forty years later, in 1928, Penicillin was invented and the population doubled again. What a day to be alive.

As an American territory, the U.P. was still dominated by the fur trade until the 1830s, as beaver and other game were over-hunted. Thousands of men could be heard saying, "We're just a bunch of trappers looking for Beaver. Where's the Beaver? Have you seen any Beaver?"

When the Michigan Territory was first established in 1805, it included only the Lower Peninsula and the eastern portion of the Upper Peninsula. In 1819, the territory was expanded to include the remainder of the Upper Peninsula, all of Wisconsin, and part of Minnesota previously included in the Indiana and Illinois Territories. After much confusion it was decided that everyone should take geography all over again.

When Michigan was preparing for statehood in the 1830s, the boundaries proposed corresponded to the original territorial boundaries, with some proposals even leaving the Upper Peninsula out entirely. Meanwhile, down state, Michigan was involved in a border dispute with Ohio in a conflict known as the Toledo War. Why anyone would want to fight over Toledo is beyond me.

The (European) people of Michigan approved a constitution in May 1835. At the time, the state government was not yet recognized by the United States Congress and the territorial government effectively ceased to exist, unlike now when they exist a little too much.

A hastily convened convention by Governor Stevens Thomson Mason, consisting primarily of Mason supporters, agreed in December 1836, to accept the U.P. in exchange for the Toledo Strip. What a freakin' deal!

The funny thing is that Ohio was considered the winner in that trade. The land in the Upper Peninsula was described in a federal report as "a sterile region on the shores of Lake Superior destined by soil and climate to remain forever a wilderness." Y'ever been to Toledo? It's a sterile region on the shores of Lake Erie destined by barges and pollution to remain forever a toilet.

When copper and iron were discovered in the 1840s, the Upper Peninsula's mines produced more mineral wealth than the California Gold Rush. Unlike the California gold rush, Michigan didn't have the fancy marketing campaign. People didn't even know about it, except in the Cornish section of England, where word apparently got out over pasties one night. Five years later, seventy-five percent of the Keweenaw was either Cornish or from Scandinavia. Sunscreen sales went through the roof.

The Upper Peninsula supplied 90% of America's copper by the 1860s. Remember, this was before there was a bunch of plastic BS. Everything was made out animal, vegetable or mineral. They even used donkeys to help cart the minerals out of the mine. Now that's an ass-load of minerals!

The Upper Peninsula was the largest supplier of iron ore by the 1890s, and production continued to a peak in the 20s, but sharply declined after word got out that Burger King in downstate Michigan had ninety-nine-cent double cheeseburgers. The last copper mine closed in 1995, although most mines had already closed decades before. By then, most other fast food restaurants had 99-cent double cheeseburgers as well.

Thousands of Americans and immigrants moved to the Upper Peninsula during the mining boom, prompting the federal government to create Fort Wilkins near Copper Harbor to maintain order. Later, someone said, "Hey there should be a couple of restaurants and some t-shirts shops, too."

The first wave of Europeans to move to the Upper Peninsula was the Cornish from England. Although they had vast mining experience, with a name like Cornish, they were considered far too silly to be productive. Then came the Irish, Germans, and French Canadians. The U.P. become a Mecca of ridiculous accents.

During the 1890s, Finnish immigrants began settling here in large numbers, forming the population plurality in the northwestern half of the peninsula, eh?

In the early 20th century, 75% of the population was foreign-born—kind of like Arizona today.

Skip to 1941. With the emergence of World War II, both the automotive and mining industries recovered. There's nothing like mass death to bolster a struggling economy.

Unfortunately, throughout the 1970s, Michigan possessed the highest unemployment rate of any U.S. state. Later, in 2009, California went bankrupt and the people of Michigan could be heard saying, "Don't come cryin' to us."

During the 70s, large spending cuts to education and public health were repeatedly made in an attempt to reduce growing state budget deficits. It didn't work. Everyone moved to Florida prompting the phrase, "Michigan—last one out shut off the lights."

Today, increasing competition by Japanese and South Korean auto companies continues to challenge the state economy, which depends heavily on the automobile industry even though everybody knows that all Ford and GM have to do is make a $\frac{3}{4}$ ton truck that gets seventy miles to the gallon.

Instead, since the late 1980s, the government of Michigan has actively sought to attract new industries, thus reducing economic reliance on a single sector. This has resulted in a series of annoying television commercials featuring actor Jeff Daniels. Well, if you're going to beg, you're going to need a face-man. What better candidate than one of the stars of the film Dumb and Dumber.

How will we ever survive?

* *The Re-Wikipe-diculous History of Michigan* first appeared in *The U.P. Magazine,* Vol 21, #7 issue, from Porcupine Press Publications.

CHAPTER VI. TRANSPLANT THIS!

I have a flag on the front of my house that says, "American by choice, Yooper by the grace of God." It's funny because I'm not from here, I'm from the south, but not really, since I was raised in the northeast. Confused yet?

Everyone always wants to know where you're from and it's tough for those of us who've lived many different places. If you ask me where I'm from, I won't tell you I'm a transplant, I'll say that I'm "American by choice, Yooper by the grace of U-haul."

If you read that right, you should at least be chuckling right now. I used that joke on stage for years so I know it works, except I used to do it in the south. The southern expression is "American by birth, Southern by the grace of God". I don't know who stole what from whom, but one of you has some explaining to do.

I have to say that Yoopers have welcomed my wife and me with open arms. I love Yoopers. They are wonderful people. And I say this because I'm about to make fun of them in this chapter. I can assure you it's in the best of spirits. What good is being a transplant if I can't entertain you?

I have a special relationship with the U.P. It's different than most transplants and extremely different than most Yoopers. One day in 2005, a booking agent sent me an email with a casino comedy tour through some place in Michigan called the U.P. The tour consisted of dates that carried me from the western U.P. to Minnesota, and I said "What the hell, I'll do it." I had some work in Indiana the following week so I figured I might as well spend one more week in the Midwest.

A couple weeks before my trip I pulled up mapquest for directions and figured out that the little strip of land between Lake Superior and Lake Michigan was actually part of the state of Michigan. I always wondered what that was on The Weather Channel. What an ego buster. You see—road comics—we pride ourselves on our extensive geographical knowledge. You drive to a couple thousand comedy shows and eventually you know the Interstates by heart. It's like a really long commute.

At the time, I had visited most of the U.S. states and was excited to go someplace I had never been. A secret little place called the U.P.— and it was loaded with wilderness and casinos and I'm an outdoors person and a comic with a casino show.

I did the shows. I drove through the entire U.P. just staring at the beautiful scenery. I did some hiking and I thought, "What a great place to live."

When I returned to North Carolina, I called the booker and told him how beautiful it was. A year later he gave me another tour, this time through the eastern U.P. I showed up at the Kewadin casino in St. Ignace with a smoking hot show and a really bad backache.

After the show, I met a girl named April. I made her laugh. She bought me a hamburger. Then she quit her job and went on the road with me. Needless to say I was pretty funny that night. Actually, she had already quit her corporate job and was just bumming around the U.P. cleaning hotel rooms and hanging out. So maybe I was just *sort of* funny.

Six months went by, and two discs in my back exploded while I was on tour in Florida. My best friend, a comic and preacher, took mercy on me and sent me back to North Carolina so I could get some back surgery. April flew down and saw me through back surgery, and a couple of months later we went back on the road for another tour.

In 2007, she moved to Florida with me. My best friend married us on the beach. We had great jobs and I had tons of comedy work, but we hated Florida. It just didn't feel safe. We said screw it let's live in the U.P. And that was three years ago. I was thirty-nine years old.

Now I'm loving my Hobby Farm way out in Ontonagon County. That's right—big shout out to Ontonagon County, and a big shout out to Houghton where a wonderful restaurant owner and his staff helped my wife and me get a foothold our first year.

So here's the question—how long before I'm a real Yooper because I definitely paid my dues to get here? In Houghton I was told that if I lived there for three winters I'd be a Yooper. The next year I bought a house in Ontonagon County and my neighbors told me I'd be a Yooper after ten winters. I guess the rules are a little stricter out in the country. AI guess the strict rules also only apply to the "local" label and not to drinking and driving. I've noticed that the further you go out in the country, the more people drive with a beer in their hand.

So they call me a transplant. So what. I've also been called a troll or a "down-stater," which is completely false. I'm not even *from* Michigan, or Wisconsin. I'm a "down-country-er." Once when I was young I got so drunk I passed out and simultaneously peed my pants. That night I was a down-spouter.

I traveled the country for years and met all kinds of folks. I have to say that Yoopers are one of a kind. But that doesn't mean they're not full of crap like everyone else. For example, I've heard this from plenty of people in the U.P.

"Oh, we don't need any of that stinkin' Lansing down there. We don't need downstate Michigan. We should be our own state—the state of Superior." Then the hockey playoffs roll around and everyone yells, "Red Wings! Yeah! Go Detroit!"

You can't say you hate downstate Michigan *and* claim the bragging rights to the best hockey team in history. I don't hear anyone bragging about the Lions.

Here's another Yooperism. "Keep it in the U.P. Shop local. Keep it in the U.P."

"Hey where'd you get those boots?"

"Wal-Mart."

Of course you bought them at Wal-Mart, they only cost thirty bucks you cheap bastard! If Yoopers could get their boots for twenty bucks from the Devil himself they'd be lining up for him like the animals did for Noah.

Yoopers aren't exactly known for their loose wallets, just ask the waiters.. Trying to get a dinner tip out of a Yooper is like trying to pull teeth in West Virginia. You might get some every now and then, but they're still pretty rotten.

That's why there were so many mines full of Scandinavian miners. They'd find a lump of copper, shove it up their butts and squeeze it into titanium. How do you like your transplant now?

Before you get mad at me, keep in mind that I spent half my life savings in the U.P. renovating the hobby farm I bought, and all that money went to Yoopers, mostly born and raised. Ouch! What a down-stater thing to say.

Y'ever notice down-staters think they can just come up here and buy anything they want? That's because they can! Everything in the U.P. is for sale. I mean everything! I've never seen so many small businesses with "for sale" signs on them. And then, after a couple of years, I realized those businesses were actually open! Gee, I wonder why things have been a little slow? Maybe because your business has been sitting around for ten years with a *for sale* sign on it!

That's a uniquely U.P. thing to do, putting a "for sale" sign on your business just in case someone makes an offer. Hey, why not? Maybe we could all just start walking around with safety helmets in case of meteor showers or wear football pads in case a game breaks out. Insert your own diaper joke here.

The point of this mess is that whether or not I'm a Yooper depends on who you ask. And the transplants don't even know. Maybe there are other transplants out there that've been here for years and still aren't sure. Well, I'm here to help. So, with that in mind I present to you:

AM I A YOOPER? (SELF TEST)

1. I have recently purchased ten pounds of bacon and/or a side of beef.

   A. Yes X

   B. No.

2. When I need things, I:
    A. Go to the store.
    B. Run up to the store.
    C. Head into town for supplies. X

3. For exercise, I:
    A. Walk a mile.
    B. Jog a mile.
    C. Walk three miles to the mailbox everyday because my four-wheeler is broken. X

4. My first child:
    A. Is a good kid.
    B. Is a wild kid.
    C. Was like eleven kids ago. X

5. When deer hunting, I:
    A. Use a tree stand.
    B. Use a ground blind.
    C. Hang out my bathroom window with a pistol. X

6. My property is:
    A. More than twenty acres.
    B. More than sixty acres.
    C. From the burn barrel to those tires down there. X

7. My backyard grill:
   A. Has rocks near by.
   B. Has lava rocks in it.
   C. Is made out of rocks. X

8. Which of the following do I say?
   A. What's the weather like?
   B. Is it cold outside?
   C. I'll be right back I have to thaw out the toilet. X

9. For my anniversary I bought my wife:
   A. Jewelry
   B. New chinaware.
   C. A bottle of deer pee and a new scope. X

10. The roads in my town are:
   A. Long
   B. Short
   C. Somewhere out there. X

11. My mailman:
   A. Is dependable.
   B. Is friendly.
   C. Can drive from the passenger seat of his car better than anyone I've ever seen. X

12. In my freezer, I have:
    A. Ice trays.
    B. A bag of ice.
    C. A cast iron pot full of frozen well-water I bash with a hammer when I'm thirsty. X

13. My driveway:
    A. Is paved.
    B. Is pebbled.
    C. Needs mowing. X

14. The last time I stepped in dog crap, I:
    A. Was mad.
    B. Was grossed out.
    C. Wasn't worried because it was just some rotten apples that LOOKED like dog crap. X

15. The pile of scrap metal in my back yard:
    A. Is getting smaller.
    B. Is getting bigger.
    C. Is my life savings. X

16. The old lady down the street:
    A. Is really sweet.
    B. Is really tiny.

C. Drives so slow that an oversized tractor-trailer hauling hydroelectric turbines actually passed her on highway 28—chaser cars and everything! X

17. My garden:
    A. Is growing quickly:
    B. Is full of vegetables.
    C. Has so much fencing around it, it looks like a prison camp for turnips. X

18. My swimming pool:
    A. Is refreshing.
    B. Is a pain to take care of.
    C. Is packed up in the shed for most of the year. X

19. My favorite hat:
    A. Is warm.
    B. Is comfortable.
    C. Makes me look like Elmer Fudd. X

20. My boots are:
    A. Snug and warm.
    B. Supportive and durable.
    C. Which ones? I have like twenty pair. X

If you answered C to more than nineteen of these, get your vision checked. Otherwise, I think the results are fairly self-explanatory. Thanks for having us in your Upper Peninsula. If you need a hand with anything just ask and we'll be glad to help. We'll probably live here for the rest of our lives, or at least until the toilet freezes over for good.

* *Transplant This!* first appeared in the Vol. 21, #8 issue of *U.P. Magazine,* from Porcupine Press Publications. You can view a copy of the original article (with pictures) at: http://content.yudu.com/Library/A1q3mb/PorcupinePressUPMaga/resources/8.htm . Click on the article to zoom in.

CHAPTER VII. ROAD STORIES

I've been a road-comic since 1993. Geographically, comedy took me many places. I lived in Hollywood for about four years, but I've never done anything significant—no big movie roles—nothing where anyone would recognize me. I managed to squeak out a gig on TV here and there as an actor, but Hollywood is fickle and the jobs were few and far between.

I left that hell in 2004 and went back on the road. That's the one thing I have done—a great many comedy shows from coast to coast. My big pay-off was that I met my wife. We're on our fourth year in the U.P. and never in my life could I have imagined I would live here.

I have a lot of West Virginia stories because I lived in North Carolina and when I traveled to the Northeast or Midwest I had to go through West Virginia to get there. I also have a lot of West Virginia stories because West Virginia is completely screwed up.

Once I was in West Virginia, waiting in line to pay for gas. The guy behind me was a big muddy guy in a white t-shirt with the sleeves cut off and an undeterminable amount of brown stuff on knee-high rubber boots. Another muddy guy walked in with a chubby kid about ten years old, and he starts mumbling something about mares for sale. I couldn't really understand him, but I'm pretty sure he was speaking English because that's what I speak and I understood *some* of it.

The big muddy guy gets a look on his face like he doesn't want to do business with the little muddy guy. He tells him there's no horses for sale because "Killer" came through to buy horses to take to Texas for the dog-food factory. He said, "They was some horses, but Killer come through." I've never looked at a can of dog food the same.

I've performed in about thirty-five states and that means I've done some driving. People have this idea about stage performers on so-called "tour"—that's what they always ask, "Are you *on tour?*"

"No."

On tour implies that I travel to places that I *want* to go to like Acapulco or The Florida Keys or Hawaii. I've been to some nice places, but I never made enough money to jet set. The bills must be paid, so my calendar generally fills up with places like Suck-boot-West Virginia, and Oh-my-God-Alabama, and What-the-hell-is-that-Iowa. That's not "on tour" that's "on the road," hence the name "road-comic"—the joke-telling version of Willy Loman.

Here's something I learned from traveling—cars catch on fire all the time. I can't tell you how many cars I've seen burning up by the side of the Interstate. I was once stuck in a traffic jam in Atlanta with about a million other idiots. Some guy's truck was engulfed in flames by the side of the road and since traffic was thick and no cops or fire trucks could get through, the commuters would have to stop 100 feet before the burning truck, wait until there was enough room beyond it, then scoot by really quick so *their* car wouldn't catch on fire. I guess that's what people mean by Hotlanta. (groan) In LA they call it a "Carbecue".

Here are a couple of other things I've learned from doing comedy shows. First of all—women are the worst hecklers. Sorry ladies, but ask any comic in the country and they'll tell you the same thing. If a man insults you in a club and you drop a burn on him, ninety-nine percent of the time he shuts up for the rest of the show. If a woman insults you in a club and you drop a burn on her, she wants to argue about it. I mean, no matter how hard the audience is laughing at her, it's like she doesn't even hear them. Even after the show is over she'll try to argue about it, with the comic—a complete stranger! Guess what? The show is over!

The worst heckler I ever had was some insane woman at a really nice military club in Jacksonville, North Carolina. I was wrapping up the show and had about five minutes left when a short old lady with a big head and giant glasses walked right up to the stage and took a picture of me—I mean, like a foot away from my face. It was a military show so I started calling her Grambo and thanked her for using a camera instead of a pistol.

She looked like E.T. so I went with it. Well, ... a highly inebriated woman in the back of the room happened to be her daughter and she didn't like that crack at all. She started blabbing at me so I did what I always do—I made fun of her. Everyone laughed, but it had no effect on her. She started shouting. So I went with the verbal A-bombs.

She stepped out of the mushroom cloud like a molten cockroach, blabbing back at me again and again—and each time I rocked her world, the audience roared, but she ignored it and tried again.

By this point, I was five minutes over my stage time and the entire upstairs audience was leaning over the balcony trying to get a look at the crazy woman they were all laughing at. She just wouldn't shut up. I told her she was a glutton for punishment. I told her I just wanted to close my show and if she would stop acting like an ass, the show would be over and we'd both probably feel better about the whole thing. Finally she said, "You think you're funny but *we're* the comedians."

I said, "Sweetheart, you're definitely something that begins with the letter "C" but *comedian* isn't the word I'm thinking of."

Standing ovation.

"Thank you good night."

What a ridiculous way to make a living.

They threw the woman out when she approached me after the show pointing her drunk finger in my face. The guy who owned the club was a Sergeant

Major named Swanyk. He invited me back four more times.

That's not to say that men don't do their share of heckling. Even though women are the worst hecklers, men are the most frequent ones—like ninety-nine percent of the time. I once did a show in West Virginia where the owner—the guy who hired me—sat right up front and heckled me for the entire show. That's right—the guy who was paying me to do a comedy show in his bar, sat two feet away from me yelling shit for sixty minutes!

Finally I said, "Herbie, shut the f&%$ up!" and the entire audience applauded. That's right—the audience applauded for the owner of the bar to shut up in his *own bar*! There's a reason people make fun of West Virginia folks, believe me, there are plenty of reasons. One day I'm gonna sell a t-shirt that says, "I got laid in West Virginia—Thanks Dad."

And so that was my life for a decade and a half—hotel/motel—it's a long way to the top if you want to rock and roll. I've since resigned to farming in the U.P, and writing. I do the occasional comedy show at various casinos and clubs in the Upper Midwest and its possible you may catch me at one of these performances. If you do—I promise you'll have a good time.

But that's such a comic thing to say. It's easy for comics to blame hecklers for all of their problems—like comics never make bad decisions. Not true—I've made plenty of bad decisions. I once shacked up with the sheriff's daughter in Lake Havasu, AZ. I didn't know she was the sheriff's daughter. It was three in the morning and we were flying down some winding canyon road. I said, "Slow down we're drunk!"

She said, "Don't worry my dad's the sheriff. We won't get arrested."

I said, "I'm not worried about going home in a police car I'm worried about going home in a hearse."

Not one of my better moments.

It's easy to watch entertainers and criticize, especially for people who've never tried to make a living as an artist. People watch TV and see Hollywood celebrities and accuse them of taking a walk on easy street and getting paid for doing nothing, but I can assure you that entertainers suffer for their art like you wouldn't believe. There will always be people who get things easily, but most artists work for free for a long time before they make any money at all.

I started performing comedy at the age of twenty-five. It took three years to get a decent paycheck and about five to make a living, barely. Then the rocky-road set in. That is, comedy became my job and I *had* to do the shows whether I wanted to or not. The bills had to be paid and so I had to drive somewhere to pay them. Imagine if your morning commute was from Marquette to Minneapolis. Let the suffering begin.

I was once so broke and hungry in Pittsburgh, PA, that after the show I walked down every floor of the hotel and picked rolls off the room service trays that were sitting outside the doors. (And this guy was making fun of West Virginia?)

I guess people don't care for their room service rolls. I recall them being quite tasty. I really had no choice. I had exactly enough money to put gas in my car and get to the next show and get paid enough from that show to get home and pay a couple of bills. Sometimes you have to book a show for low compensation in order to get to the show that pays good money.

And plenty of times shows get cancelled. Imagine waking up in the morning to this phone call, "Hi, this is work calling. Your job is cancelled next week."

Then again this is Michigan—happens all the time.

* *Road Stories* first appeared in *U.P. Magazine,* vol. 21 #10, from Porcupine Press Publications.

CHAPTER VIII. FUNGICIDE

There's nothing I like more than a good ole' fashioned casserole or as I refer to it—God's gift to the indecisive.

"What do you want for dinner?"

"I can't decide."

"How about everything all mixed up in a pan and baked in the oven?"

"Will there be cheese?"

"You betchya! I'll get some mushroom soup."

Good ole U.P. church ladies and their mushroom soup. That's what everyone uses for casseroles—mushroom soup. I've never seen a liquid thicken like mushroom soup does. Apparently when milk condenses enough it turns into Portland cement.

I'd bet you could build a house out of mushroom soup.

"What is *that*—stucco?"

"Nope. Campbell's."

According to my pals at Wikipedia—*"Cream of mushroom soup is a simple type of soup where a basic roux is thinned with cream or milk and then mushrooms and mushroom broth are added. It is well known in North America as a common type of condensed canned soup and is often used as a base ingredient in casseroles and comfort foods."*

That's why I love the Internet. It tells you all the things you couldn't figure out on your own. I always hated that saying too—"comfort foods". *All* food is comfort food because ... who's comfortable when they're hungry?

Americans always talk about food like it's a drug. It's the Food and *Drug* Administration, not the Food and Beverage Administration, like we're going to O.D. on mushroom soup.

Imagine the police breaking into someone's apartment after neighbors complained of a smell. They find a man in his recliner—dead for days.

"What killed him?" asks the sergeant.

"Probably mushroom soup," replies the lieutenant.

"How can you tell?

"Well look at how comfortable he is. He's all leaned back in that chair—the bathrobe, the bunny slippers—this guy's got comfort food written all over him."

Across the room, one of the uniforms chimes in, "Hey lieutenant, we got coupons over here—*Mushroom soup: Buy five, get one free.*"

"Where's that, Family Dollar?"

"Nah, it's the Save-a-lot. Looks like their havin' a sale."

"Okay, get down there and book 'em for fungicide."

I don't know who invented mushroom soup, but you have to be kind of whacked in the head to want milk to condense in the first place. Most of us spend our entire lives trying to *prevent* the milk in our refrigerator from condensing.

Not the mushroom soup people. They're out there every day, condensing that milk. "What is that, liquid? We gotta' thicken that. Call the flour people."

The cooking possibilities with mushroom soup are endless, too, and the soup itself has a rich, creamy history. During the middle ages, mushroom soup was used in combat when boiling oil became scarce. Plebeians at the top of a castle wall would pour scalding kettles of mushroom soup down upon their enemies, burning them in a condensed, milky death.

This became such a popular weapon that in 987 A.D., when the army of Edmond, Duke of Helfordshire, attacked rival castle Windmoor, they brought with them a giant box of green beans and French fried onions. The castle door was assaulted, the soup was dumped, and the first green-bean casserole was born. The Windmoors were defeated when the Duke and his men ate their way through the front door.

The French and Italians have used mushroom soup for their sauces and recipes for hundreds of years without much ado, but in England in 1542, Sir Thomas Crabb of Ravenscrest officially deemed mushroom soup, "The best thing to install wallpaper with." Crabb was recognized regionally as "unusually silly" and later was accused of publicly brushing elderberry jam on the ankles of wealthy women. In 1543, he was tarred and feathered and forced to wallpaper the entire new west wing of Windsor Castle.

Mushroom soup lay dormant from the headlines for several hundred years, biding its time in the culinary world. It would not break out of this hibernation until the industrial revolution when new canning technologies were invented. Sadly, it took several condensed milk tragedies before the birth of the modern can of soup.

For example, in 1895, thirty-two people were killed when a local publication held a promotional giveaway. A swimming pool was filled with mushroom soup and five horse-keys were placed inside, one being the key to a brand new buggy. Contestants had to swim in the soup and find a key. Unfortunately, the swimming pool was eight feet deep and the soup was too thick. All thirty-two people drowned in what became the first "cream of mushroom soup with people" recipe.

Several decades gave way to other tragedies including the great mushroom soup fire of 1898, the great mushroom soup flood of 1901, and the great mushroom soup hydrogen balloon accident of 1902. Lesser-known tragedies included the mushroom soup strangling of 1907, the mushroom soup gross-out of 1910, and the "holy crap I'm allergic to mushrooms" realization of 1912.

Finally, in 1934, the Campbell's Soup Company mastered the modern can of cream of mushroom soup that we all know and love today. Once released to the public, everyone hit their foreheads with the palm of their hand and said, "D'uh!" Incidentally, that is how the phrase "D'uh!" became so popular.

Mushroom soup was a big hit that year. People called each other on their telephones and said, "Hey, have you seen this mushroom soup can?"

Sadly, this mushroom soup fever would be short-lived as chicken noodle soup was released the same year. This led to the cream of mushroom division calling the chicken noodle division and saying, "Hey, you stealing our thunder over here? I'd like to see you try to condense that chicken noodle crap!"

In the early sixties, the famous artist Andy Warhol began painting Campbell's soup cans but unfortunately, he chose to paint *tomato* soup. Again, the greatest, thickest soup ever invented would have to play second kettle.

Today, the importance of mushroom soup has become two-fold. First, it has kept the farming belt fed for like a hundred years. Second, nothing is funnier than putting a full, unopened can of soup on a campfire then hiding behind a tree and waiting for it to explode. Those are the times you really remember—the exploding can of soup in the campfire times.

I was wondering about the largest bowl of mushroom soup ever eaten, but I couldn't find anything on the Guinness web site. However, I did learn that the largest commercially available *hamburger* is five hundred and ninety pounds, available from a Canadian company for forty-five hundred bucks. I bet if you ordered a mushroom and Swiss burger with fries, the cost would well exceed eight or nine thousand dollars, maybe ten with lettuce and tomato. "And could I get a side of Ranch for an extra grand?"

Imagine the beer you could have with that sandwich?

I hope they find an antidote for cholesterol some day. If they had that available now I'd eat a five hundred and ninety pound mushroom and Swiss burger every year. I'd work months to pay for that burger.

If you search for recipes that call for cream of mushroom soup you'll find a billion, but here are some of the more unusual ones I found: smoked beef mushroom soup with onions and celery; Russian Lenten mushroom soup that is based on potatoes, mushrooms, celery and carrots, and finally, the little known Farzic[1] recipe which calls for the boiling of a cat stomach that's been soaked in coconut milk and fennel for twelve parsecs[2].

As you make your way through your own universe of food, I strongly suggest you make your own mushroom soup some time. Making your own soup is fun, rewarding, and soup always freezes great for the winter. It's just like my great, great, grandmother from Scotland used to say: "inside every one of us, there's no greater comfort than the comfort of boiled fungus and condensed milk ... except for maybe a sheep's brain."

[1] Farzic — a fictional people.
[2] 12 Parsecs — the length of a race in Star Wars[3]
[3] Star Wars — a movie.

**Fungicide* first appeared in Porcupine Press Publications *U.P. Magazine*, Aug/Sept 2011 issue.

CHAPTER IX: WHY THERE AREN'T MANY MAGICIANS IN THE U.P.

I love a good magician. But I live in the U.P. and a magician's not so easy to find up here. Here's why:

1. Ate the rabbit.
2. Lost magic wand dousing for water.
3. When doves are released someone always yells "PULL!"
4. "Nothing up my sleeve trick" doesn't work because sleeves were torn off flannel shirt years ago.
5. Tuxedo doesn't fit beneath parka.

6. No "woman sawed in half routine"—broke the saw cutting up magic coffin-boxes, magic tables, magic cards, and top hat for firewood.
7. Pistol with pop-out flag that says, "BANG" turned out to be real pistol.
8. Scrapped "iron maiden" for $220 a ton.
9. Tried flying to a gig—died in wilderness attempting to find Sawyer International Airport.
10. Pawned magic equipment for "happy hour."
11. Killed by angry drunk after saying "Abracadabra," which turned out to be a Scandinavian insult.
12. Performed new trick at casino show—"watch my paycheck disappear."
13. A top hat with earmuffs and a fur cape looks ridiculous.
14. Hit a deer.
15. Lovely assistant dating someone downstate.
16. Need two hands for magic and right now one is holding a beer.
17. "Only an illusion" refers to show attendance as per bingo night, poker night, bowling night, softball night, ping-pong night, pool night, dart night—everything but magic night.
18. Couldn't escape "underwater escape trick" with six inches of ice on top.

19. Only tuxedo rental shop is ninety miles away.
20. After asking for "volunteers," audience threw a spaghetti dinner and pancake breakfast.
21. Someone said, "Slight of hand," and everyone thought, "Sleet at hand?"
22. Roommate borrowed tuxedo for shotgun wedding.
23. Best trick—audience disappeared.
24. Worst trick—turned aluminum can into a dime.
25. At end of show magician says, "Ta-da" and everyone thinks, "yeah, ta da U.P."
26. Couldn't figure out how to do "country and western" themed show.
27. Tuxedos can't exist in close proximity to penguins.
28. Charged a cover to the show.
29. Roommate used magic flash powder for muzzleloader season.

* *Why There Aren't Many Magicians in the U.P.* first appeared in Porcupine Press Publications *U.P. Magazine*, Aug/Sept 2011 issue.

Chapter X. Al Capone/Show Biz—Larger than Life

It's no secret that Al Capone spent time hiding out in the Upper Peninsula of Michigan. When I told my friends I moved to the U.P. even *they* said, "Who'd you kill?"

I'm no Al Capone, but I do find the guy fascinating. He had a serious weight problem and you just don't hear too many people talk about it. You always hear how tough he was, how rich he was, how influential he was, but you never hear anyone talk about how he may have benefited from say *Atkins* or *Nutri-system™*.

I suppose one of the benefits of being Al Capone is that you can be a big fat guy and the people around you still tell you how good you look—like actors.

Last year I watched the Macy's Thanksgiving Day Parade. The truth is, I watched the *end* of the Macy's Thanksgiving Day Parade as I waited for football to start. The credits rolled and just for kicks, I started reciting them out loud as I read, "Produced by Dave so and so, directed by Tom so and so, written by John Blank."

Written by? Do you really need someone to *write* a parade?

FADE IN:
It's Thanksgiving. Giant cartoon balloons, high school marching bands and social organizations make their way down the avenue ... uh ... you know ... like a Parade.
THE END
FADE OUT

"Hey honey I wrote a parade. That was a lot easier than that protest rally I tried to write a few years ago."

FADE IN:
A town square. A crowd has gathered. They're protesting, angry and chanting ... uh ... hmm ... what are they chanting? Dammit, what are they chanting?!

I imagine the writer of the parade living in New York City and using the credit to pick up women at bars later on that night.

"Did you see the Macy's Parade today? I wrote that. That part where the cartoon characters float around on ropes? That was mine."

No matter how weird show business is, none of it changes the fact that Al Capone was a big fatty. He was born Alphonso Caponi on January 17, 1899, in Brooklyn, New York, but later shortened his name to Al because everyone kept calling him "The Phonz".

He was one of seven children born to Gabriel and Teresa Caponi. After removing Capone from the womb, the doctor slapped him. Enraged, Capone beat the doctor to death with the umbilical cord. Capone then attended school through the sixth grade until he beat up his teacher and was then beaten up by the school's principal. With all of these beatings going on, Capone finally said, "Fuggit-about-it, lez git' some friggin scrambled eggs!" Thus, the path to high cholesterol and obesity began.

Angered by the gap between the American dream and his own starving reality, Capone began to engage in overeating and criminal activities as a way of achieving success in what he saw as an unjust and delicious society.

Word is, he started by stealing a large submarine sandwich and devouring it. The sandwich is believed to have been pastrami, capricola, ham, and salami with extra mayo and provolone on a fresh Italian sub-roll. Thinly shaved lettuce, tomato and onion were also standard at the time, but Capone is believed to have picked off all of the vegetables—even the pickles.

He worked odd jobs for a while, but was eventually hired by a gangster named Johnny Torrio to beat people up. Capone, eager to get ahead, beat up Johnny Torrio. Torrio replied, "Fuggit-about-it, kid, first day on da' job. It's our fault for not explainin' better."

Capone responded by eating two ribeyes and three whole boiled potatoes with butter, sour cream and bacon bits. Later, during a bar-fight, Capone received a razor cut on his cheek, earning him the nickname "Scarface" and eliminating any chance for the nickname, "Fatty Arbuckle".

After years of overeating and beating people up, it is rumored that Capone left New York for Chicago in order to escape a murder charge. However, this researcher has determined that the real reason Capone moved to Chicago was that he craved a pizza with a much thicker crust.

Al, "Alphonsi", "The Phonz", "Scarface" "Fatty Arbuckle" Capone just couldn't get enough of that deep-dish satisfaction. And thank God for prohibition because nothing washes down deep-dish pizza like red wine that's been fermented in someone's toilet.

The citizens of Chicago had not been in favor of Prohibition. Many of them were more than willing to break the law by purchasing alcohol. Capone took advantage of this attitude and conducted his business openly. As he would tell reporter Damon Runyon, "I make money by supplying a public demand. If I break the law, then the people in Chicago are as guilty as me. You gonna' eat them fries, Mr. Reporter?"

Capone would later comment to The New York Times, "I shoulda' eaten them fries. I knew that punk wasn't gonna' eat them fries."

Capone protected his liquor and gambling houses by waging war on rival gangs. During the St. Valentine's Day massacre in 1929, seven members of a rival gang led by George "Bugsy" Moran were shot to death in a Chicago garage. Afterward, Capone took his entire gang out for dinner where candies and several "be mine" Valentine cards were exchanged. For dinner, Capone is believed to have eaten a two and half pound ground-round with all of the toppings, mashed potatoes and gravy, and cheesecake for dessert.

Protecting his businesses also involved either beating up public officials, or bribing them with gift certificates to his chain of restaurants, good at any participating location in the tri-state area.

As Capone's profits continued to grow, he began to act as if he were a well-to-do businessman rather than a prospective spokesman for Jenny Craig™. Many people, including members of the police and city government, admired him sending him fruitcakes and other disgusting food for Christmas. Between 1927 and 1931, Al Capone was viewed by many as the real ruler of Chicago, and with a keester that huge, he was probably viewed by many others outside of Chicago, as well.

In the late 1920s, President Herbert Hoover ordered his Secretary of the Treasury to find a way to put Capone behind bars. A young man raised his hand and said, "Why don't we tie a sandwich to a string and use a stick to dangle it in front of him, then we'll lead him right to jail." This man was never heard from again.

Capone had managed to escape jail-time for any of his crimes and at this point was hungrier than ever. But his profits from bootlegging started to decline as a result of the Great Depression and the subsequent ending of prohibition. Distraught, Capone became a recluse in his penthouse eating bon-bons and watching silent films. Unable to read, Capone would exclaim, "What da' hell are they saying! I gotta' get somethin' to eat!"

U.S. Treasury agents were able to arrest Capone for failure to file an income tax return and he was later found guilty of tax fraud. This had absolutely no effect on his appetite. In October 1931, the day before he was sentenced to ten years of hard labor, Capone invented jailhouse pizza delivery service. His slogan was, "We're there in thirty minutes or it's your ass!"

After sentencing, Capone replied, "Three hot and a cot! What's for dinner?"

Sixteen years later, he died in prison in Florida at a hefty two hundred and sixty-three pounds. His last words were, "That damn reporter never ate those fries. I shoulda' killed that punk!"

And that's the beef on the chunky side of Al Capone. I have to go now because I'm hungry and I have several parades to write.

Al Capone/Show Biz—Larger than Life, first appeared in **The Drumschtick**, 2012. *(*www.drumcomic.com/drumschtick.html*)*

CHAPTER XI. URINE NATION

In Michigan's Upper Peninsula all of the houses come with at least one and a half bathrooms—the one inside and the great outdoors. In the three years I've lived in the U.P., I've probably peed outside more times than I've peed outside in the last twenty years of my life. And I see other people doing it, too. It's not just me.

One time I saw a county worker whizzing next to his highway mower like the motorists passing by wouldn't even notice.

(motorist) "Hey that guy must be very interested in something on the ground because he's just standing there looking down."

I can't say I blame him. It was eight-thirty in the morning and I had a cup of coffee in my hand as I passed him. But it just goes to show that peeing outside in the U.P. is here to stay.

I took a shortcut home a few weeks back and some old-timer had stopped his truck in the middle of the country road and was taking a whiz behind the driver's side door. Wow, great hiding place! That's pretty blatant right there, not even making any effort to stay out of sight.

At least the county worker was hiding behind his mower. I did the courteous thing of course—I laid on my horn, and yelled as loud as I could, "PUBLIC URINATOR!!" pointing my finger at him like one of the aliens in *Invasion of the Body Snatchers*.

No, I didn't do that. I did the courteous thing, though. I stopped my car at a safe distance and let him finish. You gotta give the old timers plenty of room. When the old-timers have to go, they have to go, especially if they're in the middle of a country road.

I have a farm so I generally work outside, and where there's farming there's peeing outside, that's just all there is to it. What am I supposed to do, walk back into the house with my muddy boots, take them off, walk to the bathroom, pee, flush, put my boots back on and go back outside?

I've been peeing in public for years—*especially* at work. That didn't go over so well at the restaurant job I used to have. I guess there are some jobs where you just can't whip it out. That's one of the defining terms of blue collar. White-collar people don't just whip it out at work. You never see a lawyer at the podium turn his back on the judge and say, "Hold on, your Honor, ahhhhhhh—I've been holding that one since eight-thirty this morning." (to the jury) "Excuse me ma'am." (shake)

Of course, the judge could be taking a squirt the whole time and we'd never even *know* it. Who knows what goes on underneath that counter he sits behind? They call it a bench but how do we know it's not really a toilet? Heck, the guy wears a gown! He might not even have *clothes on* underneath that thing! Who goes to work in a gown, anyway? Mental patients, ballroom dancers and judges.

We don't use weed killer on our organic farm. That's why I strategically plan out my public leaking. A little around the mailbox, the grass growing up in the sidewalks, the shaggy parts of the fence-line. Being a man is like always having a half-gallon of Roundup™ at your disposal. And it's pre-mixed so there's no messy measuring cup.

I'll tell you where I don't pee—anthills. You gotta be kind of sadistic to pee on an anthill. You're outside with nothing but farm and forest and the one place you decide to take a pee is on those poor little ants? And why? Because you think it's funny, you sadistic, anthill-peeing S.O.B. Okay, I've peed on anthills, too, but not anymore. From now on, I make a conscious effort *not* to pee on anthills. I poop on them . (just kidding)

Every living creature takes a whiz outside in the U.P., even the rocks. On Highway 28/41 around the Michigamee area, there's a tree-lined cliff where the water just shoots out of the rocks. I'm telling you, the rocks are peeing alongside of the highway in Michigamee! I suppose either they can't help it or they just don't care. (first rock to second rock) "I have to take a leak."

"Again? It didn't even rain last night!"

"Hey cut me a break! All I do everyday is sit here, staring at that lake across the street."

The more I think about it, the more I feel that a person's occupation is the biggest factor in Urine Nation. I bet firemen have to pee all day long. Plumbers? Lifeguards? Heck, why do you think lifeguards dive in the water every now and then to swim around? To cool off?

How about the sales guy at an aquarium store? What about Home Depot™? You're telling me that the guy in the bathroom section, selling those toilets all day, doesn't have to whiz about a hundred times?

I'll say this about urinating in public—it's better than throwing up in public and that's legal. Y'ever see some poor drunk just wrenching up his wounded soul inside a Waffle House at three 'o clock in the morning? "Uh...check please?"

It's gross but you gotta feel their pain. I've puked in public a couple of times myself. I had a great idea for a book title once, "*Puking With The Stars—the best places in Hollywood to puke in public when you're drunk..*"

Unfortunately, I only knew of *two* good places in Hollywood to throw up—the subway station, and behind Tommy Burger™. I also know one of the *worst* places to throw up—out of the window of a cab. I decided that if I really wanted to finish that book I'd have to start drinking more and that would be dangerous. The point is that Urine Nation is with us to stay.

One of the best places to pee in public is off the top of tall structures, a house, skyscraper, or cell-phone tower and such. If I was into that, I think my favorite place to whiz in the U.P. would be off of the old train bridge at Agate Falls. That's like a one-hundred-and-fifty-foot leak. All of the tourists down below at the observation deck would think the waterfall was spraying them.

(snapping photos) "It's so beautiful...and I can feel the spray on my face. Ooh and the water is *warm, too*!"

I honestly think a person could talk about Urine Nation for hours, but I have to go myself, so please forgive me while I step outside.

Urine Nation* first appeared in **The Drumschtick, 2012. *(www.drumcomic.com/drumschtick.html)*

CHAPTER XII. I CALL 'EM TOTS

If you live in the U.P., I'll bet you like those tater tots. I know I sure do. Remember in Napoleon Dynamite when the bully squished Napoleon's tots? That's grounds for a butt whoopin'. Where I come from, you don't mess with another person's tots.

Tater Tots made their first appearance at The Fontainebleau Hotel in Miami Beach in 1954. The Fontainebleau Hotel is a French name that in order to be pronounced correctly, requires a person to let all of the air out of their nose while simultaneously eating cheese and reciting the phrase "Fon-tain-Blue".

The hotel was brand new in 1954 and was constructed that year for the sole purpose of showcasing starches and other high-carb foods. No, it wasn't, but this was just after World War II when people and potatoes were like peas and carrots.

Other starches on display that night were potato pancakes, potatoes au-gratin, rice balls, and an entire sack of flour with a spoon inside. Needless to say, the Tater Tots came out on top, although one enthusiastic individual *did* comment that that was the best sack o' flour he'd ever spooned.

If you scour your potato history, you'll find that the official reason for the showcase at the, (say it with me) *Fon-tain-bloo-Ho-tel,* was a breakfast gathering during The National Potato Convention.

"Hey honey, we're going to The National Potato Convention, and then we're going to the world's largest ball of twine with The Griswolds. See that, kids? Big Ben, Parliament?"

I thought the convention breakfast gathering was an interesting fact because I've always enjoyed Tater Tots for breakfast, much more than lunch. Now I understand why. Isn't that what

McDonald's hash brown is, after all—a big Tater Tot?

Among the attendees at The National Potato Convention of 1954, at . . the *Ho-tel-Fon-tain-bloo*, were the brothers and founders of the Ore-Ida Company, named Nephi and Golden Grigg. They lived on the border region of Oregon and Idaho hence the name Ore-Ida—head slapper.

Nephi Grigg was nicknamed "Neef" because the name Nephi is *way* too complicated to pronounce drunk, but Neef? You could say that after ten boilermakers and a bag o curly fries any ole night of the week.

Nephi and Golden were trying to answer the same question most food company owners work on. What are we going to do with all of the leftovers? We can't eat them, we already tried that and now we look like the Goodyear Potato Blimp.

Neef came up with the idea of adding flour and seasoning to the potato slivers, mashing them up and running them through a machine that forms them into little balls, like Play-dough except Potay-dough ... ahhhh.

Of course! Why didn't *I* think of that? In fact, just the other day I was mashing up starches in my kitchen and I thought to myself, "If only I could form these into little balls via some kind of ball-maker!"

As it turns out, leftover potatoes smashed through a ball maker were a tough sell at The National Potato Convention in 1954, probably because of that snooty hotel, *The Ho-tel-Fon-tain-bloooooooo.*

The Potato people were like, "Hey, here's some taters squished through a ball maker," and the hotel people were like, "What? Potay-dough? Tots? Neef? That's not French!"

So, according to the information I researched for this article, Neef *smuggled* the Tots in. There was very little information on *how* he smuggled them in other than that he just carried in a satchel full of Tater Tots. Does this guy have great ideas or what?

I bet 1954 was awesome. Try smuggling a satchel of something into a hotel convention these days. You're going to be frisked and violated six times before your Tots even make it through the lobby.

Not back then. It was just a simple case of *The Man* trying to keep the Tots down, but instead, *The Neef* smuggled those potizzles into the convention and what do you think happened? That's right, the people scarfed the Tots and the Tots hit the big time. One person replied, "These are the best potato balls smashed through a ball-maker that I've ever had."

So now I'm thinking—it's the Upper Midwest. I own a farm. I gotta get my Tater Tot on. How the heck can I smash some taters through a ball maker myself and in the process, make myself a fortune? Here's what I did.

First I got some potatoes and boiled them. Then I cooled them down in ice-cold water. Then I patted them dry and shredded them with a cheese grater. Then I added some sautéed onions and a little flour and seasoning. Then I mixed them all up. Then I made little balls with my hands. Then I deep-fried those beauties in my little deep fryer. Then I ate those some-bitches with some ketchup and ranch dressing. Then, after it was all said and done, I decided that next time I'd just buy 'em.

All Re-ida!

* *I Call 'em Tots,* first appeared in the Dec/Jan 2011 issue of *U.P. Magazine,* from Porcupine Press Publications.

CHAPTER XIII. GETTING DRUNK—STILL FUN AFTER ALL THESE YEARS

Thursday, January 28, 2010

Twenty below, that's how cold the wind is blowing right now through my back twenty acres in Ottawa National Forest. The snow is coming down sideways and in great sheets and it's drifting up over my enormous woodpile, although the pile is much smaller than it was in November.

By my count, this is the fifth below-zero U.P. storm of the year. My wife and I are planning to ride it out with a couple of bottles of decent red wine. Okay *four* bottles. We'll be drunk in a matter of hours because it's two-thirty in the afternoon and we've already begun to sip. I can feel the false warmth of delicious red wine pouring down my chest and into my drinker's belly. Outstanding!

Now give me a chance to defend myself. I don't want anyone to get the wrong idea, like I'm just pouring wine down my gullet every day. After all, I drink beer, too. And today is a special day, a frozen blizzard U.P. day where my mission is three-fold—get drunk with wife, eat dinner with wife, go to bed with wife, but not necessarily in that order. Talk about family values!

I want you to know that I don't condone alcohol use. I simply participate in it. I don't condone messy households either, but I frequently participate in that as well.

And I know what some of you are thinking because I've seen the liquor commercials. *Please drink responsibly*. I could almost abide by that if I knew it was sincere and not just a slogan written by some lawyer who wanted to keep his client's ass out of a sling. Can you say disclaimer?

Why doesn't anyone tell you to do anything else responsibly? Please marry responsibly. Please manage your finances responsibly. Please breed responsibly. Any one of those could end in great disaster, especially the breeding! And telling a writer to *please drink responsibly* is like telling a stripper to *please keep her shirt on*. Besides, I am drinking responsibly. I'm at home.

It's no secret that people have been getting drunk for thousands of years. I've done some research on the subject and as far as I can tell, getting drunk is still just as fun as it ever was. Why are people so quick to condemn the pleasurable and dangerous? Things are tough all over and we could all use a few drinks, a little fun and some good old-fashioned danger.

The ancient Egyptians used to drink mead, a fermented honey beverage. Believe me, they didn't just sip it—they got plastered! They drank it and they built the pyramids. Did *you* build the pyramids? I didn't think so.

The Vikings also drank mead. I mean, they guzzled it. Merry making, they called it. Now, thousands of years later, they went to the NFC championship with a forty-year-old quarterback!

In the middle ages do you know who was primarily responsible for brewing beer? Monks! That's right! If you can't save 'em, serve 'em! Let him who hath a free hand chug the first mug!

My point is that there are two sides to every issue ... hold on, I just took a big drink of wine ... delicious ... and I'm tired of the negativity. I'm tired of listening to people talk about what's bad for me. You know what's good for me? Sitting inside with my wine instead of trudging outside through the blizzard!

Okay, the bad. We all know about the bad. How could we not? Every minute of every single day someone wants to tell us—please drink responsibly, say no to drugs, exercise an hour a day, don't smoke, don't litter, don't have any fun and blah blah blah.

I know there are thousands of families who have suffered great tragedy from alcohol. That's not my fault. I didn't do it. I was at home drinking responsibly. Aren't there also thousands of families who have *benefited* from alcohol? Several families come to mind; The Anheusers, The Busch's, The Lienenkugels, The Millers, The Schlitzs, the list goes on and on. Those families owe everything they have to alcohol.

Like you and me, they're just people.

And just like you and me...they're thirsty!

I don't need someone telling me to please drink responsibly. I learned that lesson the first time I *didn't* drink responsibly and woke up the next day with head-spins, mystery bruises and a headache that could split an oak.

I love my wife. My wife is the best thing that ever happened to me. One night I got so drunk I saw two of her. How beautiful they were! The only thing better than one of my wife were two! I've done plenty of jogging and it never let me see two of my wife. Maybe one day I'll see three, who knows?

There are many people who have made many poor decisions while intoxicated. There are those who would blame the alcohol: "George got so drunk he fell off his two-story deck! Alcohol is the scourge of man!"

Maybe George wasn't that bright. Maybe George wasn't a great decision maker. Maybe George didn't just lose control of himself on that deck, maybe he lost control of himself in vast other areas of his life and alcohol was just a symptom.

What about people who do stupid things while sober? Aren't these people the real threat? These are people who don't need alcohol to be asinine; they do a fine job without it! Blame the alcohol? Hold on ... (sip) (delicious) ... I think not!

Certainly no situation could be more sobering than an appearance in court. Yet, in a Pennsylvania court, the lawyer for a drug dealer pleaded with a judge to reduce his client's bail from $150,000, citing that his client wasn't a risk to flee. At that moment, his client jumped up from his seat and ran out of the courtroom! He was captured an hour later and the judge re-set his bail at $500, 000. (From: JB & Billy radio show)

Perhaps it was sobriety that allowed this young man the time he needed to think. And what did he think about? Escape!

I could go on and on about the stupidly sober but since time is limited, Google this: "Sober people doing stupid things". You'll find an endless supply of materials available on this subject, from YouTube videos to an entire Facebook page devoted to these morons.

These are the people who raise our insurances rates, the people who lower the high school curve, the people who wear orange safety vests and don't have highway jobs. Stay-at-home-drunks unite! Believe me, if we ever left the house we would!

A big gust of wind just rocked the plastic cover on my woodpile. It's one of those windy days that sting every square inch of your exposed skin. I won't know. I've already stocked a two-day supply of firewood, and wine, inside. Besides, the wind can't numb exposed skin if it's already numb from wine. Anyway, by the time I return to the woodpile it'll be Saturday and up in the twenties again.

My wife and I, and our wine, are cozy warm and getting warmer even. I'd venture to say that things were probably a lot like this hundreds of years ago—a nice wood fire, having some wine, torturing people on a big wooden stretcher, ah, the good 'ole days. Now if you don't mind, I'll be having another drink.

* *Getting Drunk—Still Fun After all These Years,* first appeared in *U.P. Magazine,* vol 21 #4, from Porcupine Press Publications.

CHAPTER XIV: FOOD OF THE GODS

There have been many stories about food from heaven, most notably in the Bible. Here in the U.P. we have our own version. The other week I had a grouse fly into the side of my house and die. Do you hear what I'm saying? A wild chicken flew into my house and died! Yes, I ate him.

Around my farm we don't eat road-kill, but we always eat house-kill. I suppose in an age of jumping Asian Carp that's not so unusual. My neighbor has about a hundred head of beef cattle. I'm waiting for the day when one of those babies walks into my house. "Steak tonight, Honey, four hundred pounds of it."

I guess that's how it goes in my neighborhood—lots of food. The wolves seem to like it anyway. Last year my same neighbor lost four of his cows to wolves. He called the DNR and they gave him a giant strobe light to put out in his field. Now the wolves aren't just eating the cows, they're throwing a rave-party afterward. Around here, that's called dinner and dancing. (male wolf to female wolf) "Do you kill here often?"

(Female wolf to male wolf) "Is that a tenderloin in your pocket or are you just glad to see me?"

I see wildlife eating their own bread from heaven all the time. In the U.P. everyone watches wildlife, even if they don't want to. I have a bird feeder in the front yard and the songbirds collect in the tops of the White Pines. One day I was pulling weeds and I saw a cannonball shoot into one of the White Pines. This was followed abruptly by the scream of thirty-some songbirds scattering in all directions. Out flew a Cooper's Hawk clutching one of the small songbirds in its talon.

That seems harsh but what goes around comes around. One day while walking through the woods I saw the remains of the same type of hawk. It looked as though it had landed and something mugged it, probably the sixty- pound cougar I saw walking through my yard last year, and when I say sixty-pound cougar, I don't mean an anorexic, horny, middle-aged woman.

Everything has to eat. That can be one of the toughest laws of the universe for us meager humans to grasp.

(Vegan) "You don't have to eat meat."

(Me) "Yes I do. If you want to squeeze soy from a plastic tube in order to feel better about yourself, go for it."

It's not that I love to kill. I just accept the law of the universe. Sure I feel bad for a cow. I got no beef with a cow. But it's not my fault they're delicious. And I think they probably know it and don't care.

Y'ever stop your car next to a cow pasture and just stare a cow in the eyes while it 's grazing? They'll look right back at you and it's like they're saying, "You can eat us, but until then, feed us until we're fat."

On this planet, humans are supposedly at the top of the food chain. Every creature has a natural enemy and the ones that don't, have man as their natural enemy. Humans are the only creatures whose only natural enemy is themselves, at least as far as we know.

Maybe that's the catch? Maybe one day extraterrestrials are going to show up and eat us?

Maybe the extraterrestrials are raising us for food, and slaughter time is about every five thousand years? If you could travel at the speed of light in the U.P, think of how many deer you could hit.

Here on the farm you learn all about the food chain. That's what farming is—your own food chain. It's busting your ass to give all of your living creatures the absolute best chance of survival—then eating them.

The mosquitoes have plenty of food around here that's for sure. My friend Lou says the mosquitoes are so big in the U.P. that after they bite you they give you orange juice and cookies and tell you to lay back and rest for fifteen minutes.

Some scientists believe that the small things are actually in charge. Humans are just servants of their every whim—servants whose only purpose is to raise those creatures, despite the fact that we eat them. We're the ones doing all the work, right? Livestock and plants don't do any work. They just sit there. We are literally slaves to our appetites!

Some take it a step further and believe that the even smaller things are *really* in charge, the viruses, bacteria and fungi. That's what cancer or a virus or dangerous bacteria are—something that eats *you.*

In that world it's all about superior numbers. When we're gone, many of those organisms will still be around, and it is only through the existence of new life forms such as us that those organisms can reproduce. We are their food. That would explain the long time correlation between food and sex—like buying somebody dinner first in an attempt to sleep with them.

Think about it. Even the words *horny* and *hungry*—they're almost the same, like *organism* and *orgasm*. Remember seventh grade biology class? Remember how the teacher would make the students read aloud from the textbook? The word *organism* showed up in the text like 84,000 times. Inevitably, some poor kid would accidentally say orgasm and everyone would laugh.

Let's face it—if love is blind, lust is Helen Keller. Anyway, food for thought.

* *Food of the Gods* first appeared in the July/August 2011 issue of *U.P. Magazine,* from Porcupine Press Publications.

CHAPTER XV. ZONED OUT

Out here no one knows what time it is. In Ontonagon County, the time zone line is only a few miles south or west and many people live in one zone and work in another. I used to live in Eastern and work in Central so I told all of my co-workers I'm from the future. One guy from Arkansas believed me.

I've been a civilian my whole life and an artist at that, and currently a farmer, so time is mostly a seasonal or daily thing to me, notwithstanding the occasional part-time job. Military people have a deeper relationship with the concept of time since they exist in precise moments. Naturally, it is the government that keeps The Official U.S. Time with something called The Atomic Clock, a device that sounds terrifying to me, like something from Dr. Strangelove.

Attempting to figure out where the time zone line is around here is another impossible task. Sure, they give us a convenient little roadside blurb that declares "you are now entering such and such time zone" but if you're on foot or 4-wheeler, forget it. Around here your cell phone doesn't even know what time it is.

So where did the time zones originally come from? Back in the old days, people were on solar time. No they didn't have active solar panels, but they did have sundials and wind-up clocks, and basically for every approximately 13 miles or so that a person traveled, the time changed one minute. Not a problem when everyone is on horseback or foot because thirteen miles is a long freakin' way!

Enter the choo-choo train. The train moves very fast and covers long distances. Now, every town you stop at, the time is different. This really put the kibosh on the lunch appointments of a man named Sanford Fleming, a Scotsman who immigrated to Canada inside a charred whiskey barrel. Fleming, a Canadian railroad engineer and egotist, decided that since the one-minute time difference was annoying to him, everyone else should change the way *they* live to better accommodate *him*. This included a set of specific time zones with a base or meridian time.

One thing that is clear throughout the early history of the United States and Canada, is that while *we* were openly taking credit for *our* inventions, there was always some other @$$hole back in England taking credit for the same thing.

In the case of time zones, it was a man named Abraham Osler who some in England call the "father of standard time," which raises an interesting question. If *he* is the *father* of standard time, wouldn't there also be a *mother*? Hmmm (chin-scratch).

The true inventor of time zones was William Wollaston, a physicist best known for reporting the dark lines in the solar spectrum and the movie Braveheart. Wollaston first came up with the idea of standardized time, but went blind from staring at the sun. "I *am* William Wollaston! They can take my eyes, but they'll never take...MY TIME ZONES! AHHHH!"

Abraham Osler took Wollaston's idea and popularized it, because he was truly a man with no life. Osler was the caretaker of the clock at the Philosophical Institute in Birmingham England, whose slogan was, "It's time to go to work, but what's the point?"

Following the sun, Birmingham is about seven minutes earlier than London. Osler made regular astronomical observations from the institute's roof and adjusted its clock. He did not suffer the same fate as Wollaston because he protected his eyes with a sweet pair of those HD Vision sunglasses—"As seen on TV!" Preserving his eyes also allowed him to sneak a peak at a publication that showed women with their dresses hiked up past their ankles—hot!

Every Sunday morning the clock-keepers of Birmingham's churches looked at the institute clock and adjusted their steeple clocks. Osler favored the new time zones with Greenwich being the standard time, but he was afraid to offer the change to the people of Birmingham because they were some rough-neck coal miners and steel workers and he was just some geek with a set of facts. So he didn't tell anyone about the time change. He just waited until Sunday morning when everyone was praying for forgiveness for all of the things they did the previous Saturday night and whammo—he made the seven-minute adjustment.

The next day when people arrived at work, late according to clocks in businesses and factories, there was much cursing of timepieces, and watch repair shops made out like bandits. No one knew that the time had been manipulated. Osler kept his secret for many years, but was found out when a man name Doc Brown showed up in a 1981 DeLorean. He and Marty McFly let the cat right out of the bag.

The railways forced uniform time and the first railway to adopt London time was the Great Western Railway in November, 1840. By 1847, most railways used London time, which was not compulsory until 1880. Many communities fiercely resisted standardized time because they hated the idea of London regulating their days.

It is interesting to note that there was almost a war over the time zones but no one could figure out what hour to show up for the battle. Shortly afterward, Osler was banished from London when he arrived late for the public engraving of a punctuality award in Piccadilly Square.

Although American references credit Charles Dowd, back in North America, Sanford Fleming was riding around on his choo-choo train striping the crap out of every available map with his time-zone scheme. At noon on November 18, 1883, North American railway systems adopted the standardized system of keeping time that used hour-wide time zones. The time zones became the official method of keeping time for the railroads primarily out of safety concerns—at least that's the story the railroads came up with, saying, "Hey, we have to know what time it is so that two trains don't end up on the same track."

And that is why, in the last one hundred and fifty years that has never happened. Ah-hemm (throat-clear). Where's Doc Brown and Marty when you need them?

It took many years, but eventually people around the world began using the same timekeeping system. However, that still doesn't explain why I'm on Eastern Time even though I live west of Chicago. Down with The King!

* *Zoned Out* first appeared in *U.P. Magazine,* Porcupine Press Publications.

CHAPTER XVI. DEPOSIT SLOP

Every spring in my U.P. farming neighborhood the snow melts, leaving behind a swath of snowmobiler and winter "booze-n-cruiser" beer cans in the roadside ditches, the likes of which I refer to as, "The Aluminum Trail."

One could very well sit around and bitch about such trash but I and a few other enterprising individuals use this time of the year instead, to ride our four-wheelers around the neighborhood and procure what I call, "a recreational paycheck."

I just love that ten-cent deposit on cans and bottles in Michigan. I've lived in states that don't have a deposit and the roadside trash really piles up. I've also lived in states with a *five*-cent deposit and Michigan has proven to me that five-cents is simply not enough money to get someone to pick up a can—in fact, it's only half enough. Sure, most states have their "Adopt a Highway," programs but one of the first things I noticed about Michigan when I moved here was the cleanliness along the highway. You see, they tell you that people have left the state of Michigan because of the economy, then you move to Michigan and there's no trash along the road and you think, "Wow, people *have* left!" Then you realize—no, it's just cleaner.

In some states, only the homeless people pick up cans. I lived in Los Angeles for four years and they don't have much of a can/bottle problem either. There are so many homeless people in Los Angeles, when you pitch a can on the ground, six people immediately dive on it in a dog pile. Fights break out. Eventually, they make some type of socialist settlement—"We'll all get .734 cents from the can, okay?" Then they ask you for a cigarette.

In Michigan, everyone picks up cans. That is, everyone who isn't doing the littering. That's the other side of the coin. Because others will pick up a can worth ten cents, some people are more likely to pitch their trash in a roadside ditch. I suppose that's just supply and demand.

One thing is for certain, you learn a lot about your neighborhood when you comb the roadside ditches. For example, someone in my neighborhood saves up all of their cigarette butts in a plastic pop-bottle (with a little pop in the bottom that I suppose they use to extinguish their butt), then, when it's full of butts and ashtray water, they screw the cap on and heave it into a ditch. WTF? Here I am picking up cans and I see one of these God-awful contraptions. Now, some kind of insane ethics question pops up: "Should I do the community a service and throw it away?"

Nope, too gross! I'll help clean up the streets for a meager wage, but I'm not wiping asses over here. At some point, the average person has to give at least *some* of a shit. I smoked cigarettes for fifteen years and I've never even *heard* of that practice.

Here's another question about the pop bottle full-o-butts: why not just litter? Your cigarette butt (extinguished please) is felt and paper—it'll decompose! Instead, you've trapped all of your *paper* butts inside a *plastic* bottle! That's a creation that'll be grossing people out for the next three million years! Can you see some poor archeologist a couple of hundred thousand years from now uncovering one of these things?

"Look! I found something!!"

"Well open it!"

"(unscrew) Oh for God's sake!"

"What? Is it a time capsule? Are there movies?"

I have to say, that's pretty lazy, and one step away from just taking a dump on the street corner. When you're out picking up cans and you see one of these things you think to yourself, "Somebody was drunk." Then you see, two, three, four or more of these things and you realize—this is somebody's life! Every day they're stuffing cigarette butts into a plastic bottle and heaving it into a ditch. I wonder what other parts of their life they've heaved into a ditch?

"But, I don't want to use my car ashtray—the re-sale value!"

Really? Peeing outside is one thing, but you're so concerned about the re-sale value of your car you'll just take a dump on the street corner? I hope to God your house isn't worth anything or we'll be swimming in feces before the end of the week!

Anyway, most of the other trash I find in the ditches is random—a milk carton here and there. I think there should probably be a deposit on cigarette *packages* because I see a lot of them. For some reason people don't feel the need to stuff their cigarette *packages* into a plastic bottle of tobacco slurry. They just throw them straight on the ground.

On a lighter note, one of the best things about the can deposit program is that it's a constant source of charity. If you need to raise money for any reason, get the gang together and comb the neighborhood for cans. My four-wheeler gets about forty miles to the gallon and when I pick, I have it worked out to about six bucks an hour—net. That's practically minimum wage!

I know, exciting isn't it? But when picking, remember to stay in the neighborhoods. The state highways belong to the adopt-a-highway program and nobody wants a turf war over the can rackets.

The point of all this is that I'm going to be cruising around my neighborhood on my four-wheeler anyway because it's fun. Why not make a couple of bucks and help beautify our surroundings at the same time? And here's the best part about picking up beer cans along side of the road. You can drink beer while you do it and no one notices. It just looks like you're picking up a can. And you are. You're picking up your *own* can, drinking it, and when it's empty, into the tub it goes. Hey, I'm just doing my civic duty.

Some other things I've found in the ditches—condoms. There should be a five hundred *dollar* deposit on those. That's how those grabber-sticks were invented, which is what I use to pick up cans—a grabber-stick. I remember when I was little kid, hanging out at my grandparents retirement community in Florida, there was an old guy who used to walk around picking up trash with a grabber-stick. Now *I'm* that guy.

Grabber-sticks are nice. though. That's one of those, "invented by an old guy" things. Young people don't invent grabber-sticks. Young people are too busy throwing condoms on the ground.

I'd like to encourage others to pick up cans this summer. Michigan, and *all* of the Great Lakes Region, is a beautiful part of the country, so don't take it for granted. I'd also like to encourage people to be more civic-minded. Complaining about the state of affairs in the country is one thing, but if you don't make the simplest effort to pitch in on even the most basic level—your own neighborhood, for example—you're just stuffing your life in a bottle and heaving it into a ditch.

Now where's my grabber-stick?

* *Deposit Slop* first appeared in the June/July 2011 issue of *U.P. Magazine,* from Porcupine Press Publications.

CHAPTER XVII. No Fly Zone

I hate to waste paper on a discussion of air-travel for the simple pleasure of humor, but the airlines continue to stay in the news, perhaps more so now than ever before. To say that jokes about airports and airplanes are cliché' is also perhaps the understatement of the century.

Perhaps other people instead would ask this question, "How many more times is this guy going to use the word *perhaps*?"

Making jokes about airlines is as cliché as it gets and yes I'm going to do it anyway, but first, a little background on something else that's constantly airborne—houseflies.

There are over 120,000 species of fly that range from one twentieth of an inch in diameter to three inches. In other words, flies celebrate diversity. Flies carry over two million bacteria on their body. In fact, it's amazing they can even get off the ground with all that baggage.

A fly's feet are ten million times more sensitive to the taste of sugar than the human tongue, giving rise to the expression, "You'll catch more flies with sugar than vinegar," although a good steaming pile of dog crap works pretty well too.

To date, no researcher has ever been able to teach a fly anything. Fish learn, worms learn, ants learn, snails learn, but not flies. This is probably why they continue to land on dog crap day after day.

Then again, they only live for twenty-four hours. How much can you really learn in a day? The clusters of flies that appear on our windows during certain times of the year attest to the fact that there are more insects in one square mile of rural land than humans on the entire earth. Also, despite having four hundred lenses in each eye, flies have bad vision, which proves my old saying—less is more. And now, some cliché comedy about air travel.

When it comes to air-travel you may as well give up on your personal freedoms. Those days are long gone. The sad fact is that no matter what the NTSB does, it probably won't work. They can x-ray your prostate and stick a cattle prod in your abdomen, but if a terrorist really wants to blow up a plane, they probably can.

I once flew from Minneapolis, MN to Hancock, MI and had a heart attack when I saw the passenger sitting across the aisle from me. She was KNITTING! With a pair of giant, fourteen-inch knitting needles that looked like they could stab a buffalo to death! Thank God for the NTSB and their no fingernail clipper policy. I feel safer.

I can see the headline now, "Knitting Needles! Red Hat Ladies Hijack Plane, Demand Trip to Golden Corral."

Here is more from the NTSB. Prohibited: knives, scissors, razor blades, guns, handguns ... (perfect) ... alcohol, wine, beer ... (losing me) ... golf clubs ... (have we ever carried them on?) ... cork-screw ... (no need without alcohol) ... self-defense sprays, pepper spray, tear gas ... (I'm with you again) ... tweezers, nail clippers ... (WTF?) more.

I don't know what "more" includes, but apparently it's not pointy, fourteen-inch aluminum knitting needles. How about my javelin, can I bring that? Maybe I could travel with a big iron hook, like the kind that lifts up car engines. We could make a movie about it: "I know what you rebuilt last summer," that kind of thing.

Sorry cross-stitchers, I'm not trying to stomp on your in-flight boredom killer. Frankly, I like the idea that you can carry them. I wish every plane were loaded with needle-pointers because terrorists don't like armed hostages. It's not that I'm scared. I just can't believe I can't carry my fingernail clippers!

It has to be a plot by the fingernail clipper people. Let's face it, how often do you really have to buy fingernail clippers—maybe once every five years? Now I have to buy them every time I land. An even worse scenario—what if people stop clipping their fingernails?

"Excuse me, may I squeeze by you?"

"Ow!"

"Oh I'm sorry, was that your retina? It's these twelve-inch fingernails of mine, they're really hard to handle."

"Hello, Guinness book of world records? I have a planeload for you!"

I later found this to be included in the NTSB "more" category: "Strike-anywhere matches are forbidden but one book of safety, non-strike anywhere matches *is* permitted," like the kind the bomber flying into Detroit tried to use. I think the message is clear, "Terrorists, if you're going to light a fuse you must first close cover before striking."

Has life become this complicated? Have we arrived at a point in time where we're so preoccupied with minutia that the obvious is regularly overlooked? It reminds me of the guy who can't find his sunglasses because they're sitting on top of his head.

"I can't find my sunglasses."

"Yeah, scratch your head while you think about it."

Here's the latest remedy: no printer cartridges. Whew, safe at last!

Flying is such a downer now. Everyone is guilty until proven innocent. I'm pretty sure that somewhere in the Bill of Rights there's something about how American citizens can't be randomly searched. In the last ten years between the war on drugs and the war on terrorism, I've been searched randomly about a dozen times. Tell people this and they're likely to say the same thing, "Well. times have changed."

Spoken like someone who doesn't wipe.

"You smell terrible."

"Yes, I recently went through some changes."

"Oh?"

Well, what are you going to do—vote? Yeah that'll work!

Terrorism aside, flying works pretty well, but only if you're taking a long trip, otherwise you're just going around your elbow to get to your ankle. I was once planning to drive to New York from North Carolina with my father.

I was living four hours south of my father's house so instead of driving the four hours to his house and then getting in his car and driving twelve hours to New York, we decided to save some time by booking a short, one-hour flight. I grabbed a puddle jumper from Wilmington to Charlotte and waited for my connection to get me to my father's house exactly ninety miles from the Charlotte airport.

I checked the monitor. Delayed one hour, then two, then three, then the bad news: "sorry folks, the flight is cancelled. Then the really bad news—there are no other available flights, we're going to put you on a bus.

Another hour or so later we boarded a bus to make the ninety-mile drive, which of course, by bus, takes about three hours. So, seven hours later I arrived at my Dad's house—three hours longer than if I just would've driven.

That's not to say that driving works all that well anymore, either. I remember back in the seventies and eighties how Los Angeles had the worst reputation for gridlock. Now every city has it: Tampa, D.C, Atlanta—the worst.

"Break out your cattle-prods, I'm flying home for the holidays!"

"You are?"

"Perhaps!"

* *No Fly Zone* first appeared in *U.P. Magazine,* Porcupine Press Publications.

CHAPTER XVIII. SEPTOBERFEST

I love hunting. I did some research on the word camouflage. It's a French word that means to use cryptic coloration or otherwise break up your outline.

I once saw a Yooper who was four hundred pounds in full camouflage—head to toe. Let me tell you something. You can't break up *that* outline. When you're pushing four hundred pounds you might as well just hunt in a tuxedo. Go ahead and walk around in a scuba suit and flippers because it doesn't matter. At four hundred pounds the trees are now blending in to *you*.

Y'ever fall asleep hunting? I do that all the time. That's the finely-tuned stalker I am. Last year I fell asleep beneath an apple tree with a loaded twenty-gauge, hammer pulled back, no safety. And they say never wake a sleep *walker*. You darn sure better not wake a sleep *hunter*. I'm pretty sure that's how wake-up calls got started.

"Go wake up Hoffman."

"He sleeps with a loaded gun!"

"Hmm. Hire a messenger."

I love fall for football season, too. Football and hunting—it's a total male overload.

Don't even get me started on Oktoberfest. The U.P. doesn't even celebrate it in October. You know it's cold when a region celebrates Oktoberfest in September. Maybe we could start celebrating Thanksgiving in July? If there was a football game on, I probably would. Football is that addictive.

Every year during football season in Green Bay, the blimp pulls back for a shot of Lambeau Field and it's like more people are wearing fluorescent orange and camouflage than green and yellow. I think fluorescent orange and camo should be the Green Bay Packers' colors.

"Donald Driver—all alone in the end zone—touchdown!"

"That's right, Bob, they just couldn't see him in that grid-iron camouflage. He blended right in to the goal line."

"Steve, it's called "still-catching." Of course if this were an away game he would've been wearing his fluorescent orange."

I grew up hunting in Pennsylvania then moved to the beach for about twenty years, so I'm trying to catch up for time lost in the forest. Everyone hunts for different reasons. One thing I love about hunting is that it forces you to ask yourself ethical questions. Some guys are trophy hunters, others will tell you that you can't eat antlers and some guys enjoy the killing a little too much.

I'm definitely in it for the food. I have no problem with killing something to eat. I don't think paying someone else to kill your food for you is any more civilized than killing it yourself. Having spent a great deal of time in and out of the restaurant world, I've seen a ton of food wasted—whole steaks in the trash.

People are just too distant from their food. I think if every meat-eater killed something once in their life they would appreciate it more. Come home empty-handed sometime and don't eat at all—then you'll really appreciate it.

Maybe we should issue domestic meat-eater licenses? When a person turns eighteen if they want to eat meat, all they have to do is go to a slaughterhouse, look a cow right in the eyes and whack him with a bolt gun, or ring the neck of five or six chickens. "You're all set, son—enjoy you're dinners."

Fall is a total overload that's for sure. And then they want to cram in all of those holidays, too. The holidays are perhaps the weirdest stretch of time during the entire year—Halloween, Thanksgiving and then Christmas. It's like Satan, Family, and then God, in that order. Act like a sinner in October so we can ask for forgiveness in December, then get drunk on New Year's Eve and forget about the whole thing.

Halloween is without a doubt the most dangerous holiday of the year, too. People spend all year telling their kids not to talk to strangers then send them into the streets to collect apples loaded with razor blades. "Have fun kids! Trick or treat!"

Fourth of July is another dangerous holiday—alcohol and fireworks, there's a real family event. They call it Independence Day because a quarter of the population ends up with fingers independent of their hand.

Overall, Thanksgiving is my favorite holiday because once you get past the football and hunting it's generally a pretty safe holiday. Unless you eat too much, then it's only dangerous for the people around you. "Watch out—Dad's gonna blow!"

Dad always overdoes it on the food pile. He puts down one layer then he builds an upper deck on top of it. "Hey dad, your stuffing is getting a nosebleed."

And so here we go again, we snap into the season and the coats pile up on the rack and the boots pile up underneath it. Wherever you hunt and whatever you hunt, may you be safe and prosperous on your travels. If you see someone in an orange vest sleeping under an apple tree —don't wake me up!

* *Septoberfest*, first appeared in the Nov/Dec 2010 issue of *U.P. Magazine*, from Porcupine Press Publication.

CHAPTER XIX: ROAD KILLIN' ME

It's that time of year again in the U.P. As you travel down that desolate two-lane road on your way to work or to your camp, a blip appears on the horizon. It's a pedestrian. You draw closer. It's not a pedestrian. It's a cyclist. He's peddling like he's in a race, but there's no one else around.

He's wearing a skin-tight, shiny, aerodynamic cyclist outfit with a teardrop-shaped helmet that reminds me of the Sleestaks from "Land of The Lost." If you ask this person why they ride their bicycle in this manner they will undoubtedly answer, "Because it's fun and it's great exercise".

Fun? Okay. But my question is this: If you want to ride your bicycle for exercise then why are you wearing that ridiculous aerodynamic clothing? Shouldn't you being wearing heavy clothes to provide more resistance and thus more exercise?

Just once I'd like to see one of these guys wearing a wetsuit with a parka on top. How about a suit of armor and a backpack full of bowling balls? Now we're really exercising! And forget that sleek racing bike, you need to ride something heavy so you can pull things, like a plow. Horses don't need ridiculous clothing to get exercise.

My theory is as follows; the real reason people wear ridiculous clothing for their particular sporting event is simply because they like dressing up. Why do you think baseball coaches wear the uniform? It's not like they're going to play. Even if the coach were a former player there would have to be a record number of injuries during a baseball game in order to call his lazy ass into action.

The same thing goes for the snowmobilers. Half of them are racing professionals with sponsors who pay them to wear those clothes, and the other half of them just like to dress up in a big fluffy sleeping bag and drink beer. Watch someone who *rents* a snowmobile sometime. They can't even *walk* in the dang suit. It's like they have hemorrhoids. Of course, if it's their first time on a sled they probably do.

I don't want to come down on all of the bicycle people because some bicycle people actually are out there pulling heavy things. The closest I've seen to this type of bicycle exercise would be those long distance cyclists. They carry luggage on their bike and pull a trailer. Now that's what I'm talking about!

Y'ever meet one of those people? I ran into a guy in a bar one time and after a couple of minutes he broke the ice.

"How's it going?"

"Not too bad," I said. "I'm kind of tired from working all day."

"I know what you mean. I did some bike riding today."

"Oh yeah? Where'd you go?"

"From Wausau to Houghton."

"Wow! How long did that take?"

"About sixteen hours."

"On a bicycle?"

"Yep."

"When was the last time you saw your testicles?"

"Somewhere back in Missouri"

You'll start meeting these people in the summer months. In the winter months they're still down in Arkansas with a full set, working their way up to soprano. Regardless of the pitch of their voice, it's good solid exercise.

Still, I have to ask, why do these people want to spend their free time in traffic? I commend you on an incredibly long bicycle ride, but let's face it, you were breathing car exhaust the entire way. Haven't these people ever heard of a mountain bike? Am I the only one that likes the woods and hates breathing car exhaust?

Here's another summertime oddity in the U.P.—pedestrians on state highways. Pardon the pun, but something retarded is afoot. Haven't these people ever heard of a hiking trail?

A person works all day and then it's time to relax with a nice walk. Do they walk through the woods and enjoy the scenic wilderness that the beautiful U.P. has to offer? No. They walk with their fat butt on the right shoulder of state highway twenty-six! If you're going to be a moron at least do it on the LEFT side of the road. And joggers—don't even get me started.

As usual, there are exceptions to every rule. Some of these pedestrians aren't out for exercise they simply don't have a car and need to get to the store, which is of course, several miles away. If this is the case then perhaps these people should refer to the bicycle section above. Some guy rode a bicycle from Wausau to Houghton and you can't find one to ride up to the BP to buy frozen burritos? The Lord only helps those who help themselves. Believe me, hell is full of morons.

Here's my idea of what Hell is really like:

You're in line at a convenient store. You want to buy an orange juice, that's it. There are only two people in front of you, another guy with a bottle of orange juice and some moron with a backpack full of lottery-tickets. You should already be back in the car by now, but the line hasn't moved because the moron has his lottery tickets spread out all over the counter and he's trying to sort out his three dollar winners from his one dollar winners even though he only has about fifteen bucks coming to him and he spent about ten grand on the tickets. The clerk doesn't care because she's on the phone trying to explain to her boyfriend Todd how to change the diaper on the kids that aren't even his. Normally, this would only take about three minutes but this is Hell, it's been three weeks. The clerk is still on the phone, but it's no use, Todd is a moron and undoubtedly back at their trailer covered in baby-poo. The lottery guy isn't just fumbling with his tickets anymore, he's starting to stink and mumble. The air conditioning inside the store turns on, but fails. It puts out just enough air to blow a whiff of the lottery guy in your sad direction and when you try to leave the store you automatically appear back in line. The guy in front of you turns around and asks you if your orange juice is warm now, too. "Yes," you reply. Suddenly you realize that he must also be new to Hell. The clerk hangs up. The guy in front of you turns around and smiles, relieved. But the phone rings and it starts all over again.

In the meantime, during your stay here on Earth, get off of the state highway and get out on the trail because the rest of us are waiting in line to buy orange juice.

* *Road Killin' Me* first appeared in *U.P. Magazine,* vol 21 #7, from Porcupine Press Publications.

CHAPTER XX. RADAR LOVE

The damage assessment came in immediately—complete overhaul. It was a small house with a big separate garage, both fairly dilapidated and sitting on a perfect twenty acres. My wife and I bought the place and started repairing it the day after closing. We knew it would be a lot of work but that's how it goes if you want to build your dream farm in the U.P.

I sat on the filthy counter of my disgusting kitchen that first day, drinking coffee with my wife who paced all around. Her brain was flushed full of remodeling ideas. My *wife* had found the ad for the house on the Internet, so I hadn't actually read it until that very moment.

The ad read: "Fixer upper. High and dry. Twenty acres. With microwave."

I had to laugh.

Can you imagine my friends asking me about the place?

"Hey Dale, how's the house?"

"It needed fifteen thousand dollars worth of repairs, but wow, what a microwave!"

If there are real estate ads in Hell they're probably written the exact same way: "For sale. House in eternal damnation. Seven hundred and fifty degrees farenheight. With microwave."

I told my friend about it and he said to me, "Well you bought the place didn't you? I guess it worked."

Yeah we really fell for it. The microwave was without a doubt the single most important factor in our decision to purchase the property. Imagine our fateful conversation.

"Honey, we fell for the oldest trick in the book—*with microwave*!"

"It's not our fault, Sweetie. The microwave clouded our vision with its plastic wood panels and it's automatic defrost setting. Who would even notice that the house needed windows, siding, and floors? We never had a chance! Another big time swindle by a crafty U.P. real-estate agent."

Since then we've completely remodeled the ground floor, painted and sided the exterior, and performed numerous ground clean up and lumberjacking details. We're almost finished remodeling the upstairs, and the garage will get overhauled this summer as well. I have to admit, I've used that microwave about a million times.

That microwave has been an essential part of our existence in Ottawa National Forest. It's a rural setting, so the freezer gets loaded. Between hunting season and the bi-monthly trip to the grocery store, the freezer in my basement is packed. If you're like me and you have other things on your mind, once in a while you'll forget to take some meat out of the freezer in advance. There's only one way to defrost meat quickly; *with microwave*, that's right, *with microwave.*

I'm a big man and I can admit when I'm wrong. Sure I made fun of it. I laughed in Mike's (that's what we named it) face. I was wrong about the ad. The ad was perfect. The only bonus while performing all of those repairs was that stinking microwave. The ad didn't say "With water heater" or "With refrigerator" and you can guess why. That's right, they were the first things I replaced.

I'm living life like it was meant to be, brothers and sisters. I'm out here in the woods with nothing but the sound of the wind blowing through the fan in my microwave as it defrosts another butt roast. It's a peaceful melting sound, like a highly irradiated spring day. I can hear the birds outside whistling in harmony as the second timer ticks down, twenty-nine, twenty-eight, twenty-seven, twenty-six.

In a just a few moments I'll be ready to slow cook the ass-end of a pig and my crock-pot is just sitting on my resurfaced counter looking at me as if to say, what about me, jackass? I'm tired of this crap! I cook the food. Mike just defrosts it! What can I say? You weren't mentioned in the ad.

It's going to be another beautiful summer in Da U.P. at my newly remodeled house and property. The fall will come again and along with it, hunting season. The grouse, rabbits and deer will escape for the most part, but a few will end up in my freezer. I'll be working on other projects by then, my wife and I a little more comfortable in our secret hideaway.

I'll take a shower with the water heater we purchased and I'll open the refrigerator we purchased only to find it empty for the day. I'll make a quick trip to the freezer we purchased, and return with some unknown hunk of meat we purchased or shot. Fifteen minutes later, I'll hear a beep and I'll remember all of the reasons we bought this little farm in the first place. We'll eat and we'll celebrate and we'll talk about how much we love our farm, the little diamond in the rough—the one that came with the free microwave.

* *Radar Love*, first appeared in *U.P. Magazine*, vol. 21 #5, from Porcupine Press Publications. You can view a copy of the original article (with pictures) at: http://gb.zinio.com/page/?issue=416125507&pg=59

CHAPTER XXI. SCAR-FACED LIAR

When I was sixteen-years-old, I ran through a sliding glass door for the simple reason that I couldn't see it. I thought it was open.

Apparently I was mistaken. Two hundred and forty-three stitches, twenty-seven staples, and twenty-some odd years later, sliding glass doors are covered in safety stickers to warn people of closure and if that's not enough, they're even made with a type of safety glass that shatters into thousands of tiny, round-shaped pieces. Myself and about a gazillion other people are the reasons why.

Back in my teenage years, sliding glass doors were made out of thick, double-paned plate-glass and when they broke, they came down in giant, cut-your-head-off-size pieces. I managed to keep my head, but my face led the way and my arm followed. Fortunately, the scars on my face were small and located in convenient, "natural face-line" kinds of places so I didn't end up looking like a waffle, but my arm suffered a large laceration that left a sizeable scar. It was one of those, "Dude, I saw all of the stuff inside my arm..." moments.

When I first returned to school after the accident, covered in bandages, there was a brief period of, "Whoa! Were you in a car accident?" and all sorts of "whats" and "whys." But then the worst thing imaginable happened—the local newspaper got a hold of it and ran an article that featured my lacerated self along with the three friends who basically saved my life, the title of which was something along the lines of, "First-aid class pays off immediately for three life-saving geniuses as their moron-friend runs through a closed, sliding glass door ... ."

This resulted in school-wide publicity for me at sixteen years of age—and me with no publicist to call. For the next year, I was no longer greeted with wonder and astonishment. I was greeted with, "Hey it's that moron who ran through the door ... ."

and any creative variation that high-school kids can think up. At sixteen years old it would seem that my entire existence had led to nothing more than a bloody, stupid-human trick.

That summer, with the scars not nearly faded, I realized that when I met new people they would immediately ask me about my arm and I learned something: making up lies about scars is super fun.

"What happened to your arm?"

"My neighbor tried to run me over with a lawn mower."

"What?!"

"Yeah, he's doing twenty years, you probably saw me in the paper."

"You know I think I *did* see you in the paper."

"Yeah, you did."

This was the true beginning of my creative writing career. Back at school, things were looking up for *Mr. Glass*. I attended a moderate-sized high school but every now and then I'd run into someone who didn't know about the door.

"What happened to your arm?"

"Flipped my dirt-bike jumping over my house."

"Really?"

"Yeah, it's a ranch-style but still ... that's a pretty good jump."

One time on a date, I told a girl that a pit bull grabbed on and wouldn't let go. I recall that being a pretty good date, and my luck was about to get even better. During my junior year, my father was offered a better job and my family moved to a different state. This meant doing my senior year at a brand new school—a big school—normally a nightmare for a high-school kid. Not for Mr. Glass.

Going to a new school means meeting strangers every day! For two months, almost every single person I talked to was a stranger. I would shake hands, they would look at the fresh scar on my arm, then ask what happened.

"You were mugged?"

"Yeah, there were eight of 'em."

"Where are you from again?"

"Pittsburgh. It's a tough town."

Boy did I roll on that one. I mean that was my go-to. After I managed to make some friends and let them in on it, "Hey guys, I didn't really get mugged, I'm just a moron who can't see glass," they started making up the lies for me.

"Hey this is Dale, he's from Pittsburgh, see that arm? Some serial killer tried to cut it off with a chainsaw!"

"What?"

"Yeah, he almost died, but he stabbed the guy with an ice pick. Up in Pittsburgh they have lots of ice-picks just lying around!"

The lies started piling up. Eventually they just became a part of my personality. Like peanut butter and jelly, scars and lies just go together.

"What happened to your arm?"

"Tore it on a flagstick in a slalom skiing competition."

"Really?"

"Of course, or in this case, off-course."

The year passed, graduation came and it was on to college. College freshmen year is just like being the new kid at high school except that *everyone* is the new kid.

"What happened to your arm?"

"Fourth of July."

"You blew up your arm?"

(nod)

And not just freshmen year, every year at college you meet new people—for four freakin' years! My college was in a coastal community and I started surfing that year.

"What happened to your arm?"

"Shark, barracuda, sawfish, underwater piling, coral reef, stingray, man-o-war, boat motor, run over by jet-skier, parasailing accident, severe sunburn—they actually had to operate!"

After college I went out into the world and found new arm-lies wherever I went. In Los Angeles, I was attacked by Scientologists. In Florida, I was the victim of a hanging chad. In Texas, Mexico did it...remember the Alamo? In Virginia it was the D.C. Sniper—the bullet ripped through my arm and bounced off a gas pump. In fact, that's how they caught him.

In New York, I had improperly prepared pufferfish, my arm swelled up so big they had to cut it open. In New Jersey, it was the mafia, in Alabama it was the KKK. In Spain, I tried to explain to a man in a hostel that in America the street gangs are so tough that everyone has a scar like that, but I think what I actually said was, "My mouth is full of hot sand and barley-malt."

In Arizona, I got hung up on a cactus. In The Rockies, it was a dang mountain lion. Once, in Kansas, I actually told the truth—I ran through a glass door. They didn't believe me.

Now here I am—a middle-aged man in a brand new state called Michigan and a whole new world of Michigan lies has opened up for me.

"What happened to your arm?"

"Bear, wolverine, badger, raccoon, skunk, eight-point buck in windshield, logging accident..."

If only those mines in the U.P. were still open. I'd love to tell a good smelter story. "Yeah, that melted iron is so hot, the flesh just fell right off my arm—you should've smelt it!"

It's not easy lying about the same accident for twenty years. You have to be creative. Whenever I get in a rut I just make three hats. In one hat, I put a reason to be in a hurry—for example, late for work or family member in hospital.

In the second hat, I put the names of places: Toys-R-Us or gas station. In the third hat, I put the names of dangerous things: cobra, sand blaster, crab-fishing boat. When there are about twenty in each hat, I start choosing.

"What happened to your arm?"

"I was ... trying to get to a wedding, but was ... crushed by a log-splitter ... in Applebee's."

That's a real conversation starter. You have to keep records, though. You can't tell a person you were on your way to donate emergency blood when your were slashed by a tarantula in Wal-Mart, and then come back a few months later and tell the same person you were answering a volunteer fire-fighter call when you were clipped by a rototiller at the mall.

You have to write these things down, "June 4: told a clerk at the grocery store that I was fleeing a tornado siren when my arm got caught in a dough-mixer at the Ford dealership."

One of these days I'm going to write down every single lie I've ever told about my arm and I'll probably have a book. I'll call it *An Armload of B.S.* But for now I'll just keep thinking up new ones. Here are some of my new Great Lakes lies that I'm considering.

-You know those zebra mussels? They're much more invasive than you think—pulled one out of my arm.

-A thirty-below wind chill fused my wet sleeve to my arm and they had to remove it.

-Bridge-fest in Houghton. Crazy.

-Fell into the Soo Locks and was pulled to safety just before the giant freighter crushed me. You can see the outline of the anchor right here ... .

-Dog-man. Crazier than bridge-fest.

-Asian carp flew out of lake Michigan and caught his tooth on my arm. You can see the outline right here...

-Oktoberfest at Frankenmuth—drank a hole in it!

-Cherry pickin' in Traverse City. Picked my arm!

-Went to Detroit!

As you can see, it's always a work in progress. So what the heck, Michigan. As I travel around The Great Lakes, I may run into you. Just remember—when the conversation turns towards mutilated flesh, I'm just pulling your arm.

That reminds me, I have leg scars, too!

* *Scar-Faced Liar* first appeared in *U.P. Magazine,* Porcupine Press Publications.

CHAPTER XXII. RANCHO KOOK AMONG US

If one is to discuss the finer points of Yooper-life, at some point in time they must discuss Ranch Dressing. No one guzzles Ranch like a Yooper. Even in the south where the creamy condiment has earned the title, "Redneck Ketchup," I think they're still a few sauce cups behind Yoopers.

In the U.P. there is no need for a fancy nickname like "Redneck Ketchup." Ranch is simply a staple of the dinner table, like potatoes or corn.

Take the average Yooper's fridge—odds are there isn't any salad in there, but there's probably a twelve-pack and a bottle of ranch dressing just waiting for fries and wings.

Ranch dressing comes from Santa Barbara, California. In 1954, Steve and Gayle Henson opened a dude ranch called The Hidden Valley Ranch. Because their last name was Henson and they lived in California, everyone thought they were related to Jim Henson, creator of The Muppets. This was completely false as Jim Henson once responded, "I don't even like salad dressing, although several of my Muppets do."

Visitors to The Hidden Valley Ranch would spend their time horseback riding, taking in the scenery, and whispering to each other about the funny Japanese tourists on the horses ahead of them. But at the end of the day when the meals were cooked, people just couldn't stop talking about the unique taste of the buttermilk salad dressing that was served at the ranch. As in, "Hey those Japanese tourists were pretty funny, but that buttermilk salad dressing could crack an engine block!!"

As more and more people began to visit the Hidden Valley Ranch and taste the flavor of this wonderful dressing, word spread like buttermilk.

One of the guests requested to take a large batch of the dressing with him to Hawaii for a party he was hosting and Steve Henson agreed. Soon the guest wanted more because everyone in Hawaii was now addicted to Hidden Valley Ranch dressing. In Hawaii, a bill was drafted to change the name of Hawaii to "The Island of Ranch Dressing," but died in the state legislature after several French dressing lovers were voted in under suspicious circumstances. By now, Steve Henson probably owns Hawaii.

Steve realized he had a great product and wanted to expand on his success. He hired illegals at the ranch so they could sell a powdered mixture of the herbs and spices used in the Ranch dressing. They offered to backpack it across the border for him, but Steve said, "Hey, it's not that kind of powder. You mix it with buttermilk."

The problem with the powdered packets was that it required users to mix it with their own buttermilk/mayonnaise combination and many households did not keep buttermilk on hand, so someone called the Amish on the one phone they own. Thousands of Amish Kinsmen heard the news and exclaimed, "Hooray! They're buying the buttermilk. We've been trying to get rid of this crap for years!"

Steve Henson decided to sell the Hidden Valley Ranch brand of dressing in 1972, to the Clorox Company for eight million dollars—coincidentally, the 1972 market value for the island of Hawaii. Clorox took over production of the milky salad-dip and decided to change some things to make the soupy sauce more easily usable for consumers.

For starters, they added bleach. Just kidding, they added butter flavoring to the mix so that users would not have to mix the herbs and spices with buttermilk. They could use plain milk instead. Someone called the Amish. They were outraged. They planned to picket the Clorox company, but lost their permit because they arrived several weeks late due to travel delays, mostly stemming from a shortage of hay.

In 1983, sales of the liquid really soared when a shelf-stable bottled version of the dressing became available. At this time, the new rage was bottled salad dressing that did not have to be refrigerated and Hidden Valley Ranch was one of the new products available. Clorox added preservatives to the recipe to keep the dressing shelf stable for up to 150 days, the average consumer's life expectancy after ingestion.

The shelf stable version just didn't hold up. Like *Flock of Seagulls*, people soon realized that the idea was short-lived and that they were just trippin' and that Jerry Garcia really *is* dead. Things went back to being the original way. The Amish were extremely excited about this, but unfortunately did not hear the news until just last week because no one called them, so a Chinese buttermilk company got the contract instead.

Ranch dressing has become incredibly popular, overtaking the more common salad dressings such as Italian, Caesar, and Thousand Island, as well as the less common Venetian, Poncho Villa and Dozen Island dressings.

One of the reasons for its success was that in the 1980s, mayonnaise was at the top of its game and Americans completely approved of its use in just about everything, as opposed to now where people want to whine and cry about low fat this and low-cal that.

Popularity soared when American restaurants began using Ranch dressing, increasing the demand for the gooey, snot-like afterbirth. Ranch soon began to be used as a dipping sauce on burgers and sandwiches, as a flavor for chips such as Ranch Lays, and as a lubricant for sex and two-stroke engines.

Ranch is now a common household name like Linda, Tom, Joe or Crab Rangoon. Not only is regular Ranch available, dozens of other salad dressing companies have created their own version. Some people have even named their kids Ranch and Buttermilk. Although Hidden Valley Ranch is the original Ranch dressing, varieties can be found such as Cucumber Ranch, Bacon Ranch, Spicy Ranch, and of course the less popular Porn Star Ranch, Cat-fart Ranch and worst of all—Fat Free Ranch. Yuk! The dressing is now sold in more than 30 countries around the world but who cares about them? This is America! Pass the Ranch!

* *Rancho Kook Among Us,* first appeared in the Jan/Feb 2011 issue of *U.P. Magazine,* from Porcupine Press Publication.

CHAPTER XXIII. FREE PRIZE IN THIS BOOK!

I don't know who you are, but I want to congratulate you and thank you for reading this. The mere fact that you are holding this written work in your hands is a credit to you. One thing I love about the written word is that it's exclusively for people who read.

As a professional comedian I can assure you that any idiot, literate or otherwise, can and will show up at a live comedy show. That's kind of the problem with live comedy. Ninety-eight percent of the audience is having fun except for the two morons in the back who aren't smart enough to shut up. Printed words like these pretty much rule out morons like those and that's refreshing.

The fact that this is a printed page and not a blur on a computer screen is something else to your credit (but if it is, I understand). Reading on a computer screen just isn't the same as holding the words in your hands where the words come alive. So congratulations my literate, book-holding friend, you are well worth the task of entertaining.

As a professional comedian, I also want you to know that U.P. Magazine (where this article and many others in this book first appeared) is more than just a local publication—it is a *humor* publication. That means the people who publish the mag are dedicated to making you laugh and that's very special.

Look around the grocery stores and convenience store stands in the U.P. and try to find another humor magazine. You won't find one because it's not there. We all know what *is* there—stories about the Edmund Fitzgerald, best places to find whitetail and catch walleye, and how much copper they yanked out of whatever mine. And it's all weaved around real estate ads and boat dealerships and other boring stuff. Surely they serve a purpose, to provide information and advertising, but U.P. Magazine is about more than information and advertising, it's about fun.

Take it from someone who's been around, you can go to another area of the United States with ten times the population of the U.P. and still not find a humor publication like the U.P. Mag. These days, most humor rags are circulated on college campuses and are very underground and targeted at pot-smoking twenty-year-olds.

That's fine, but I'm forty-two and knee-deep in the stuff of life. For me, comedy is about middle-aged people with jobs and problems. For example, y'ever fart in the shower and suddenly realize you're standing in a small, enclosed area? I did that one time and almost choked to death. My wife got out. We shower alone now. This is the written intellectualism I'm referring to.

In the age of digital everything, nobody really knows what will happen to the printed word. Newspapers are already starting to experience declines in circulation. They're attempting to make up the difference with Internet ad dollars but it hasn't made the difference. It's just easier to watch TV.

I like to read because it's exercise for your brain. There are computer books now that you "flip through" on your I-phone or Blackberry or whatever device you stuff your pockets with. That makes no sense to me. Anyone over thirty-five remembers their parents saying, "Don't sit too close to the television set. It's bad for you."

Now we carry the TV around in our pockets. That's pretty damn close. The rest of the time we're glued to some type of home computer screen. In fact, I'm staring at a laptop right now. It's about a foot and a half away from my face. Oops.

What am I going to do, start buying whiteout again? I may be suffering from radiation burns, but at least I can print this article on paper and hold it in my hands or better yet, give it to someone else who can.

So again, I congratulate you for holding this book in your hands. You've joined an elite group of people who have learned to laugh at more than just television and film. You have joined the world population of funny readers.

Now please, read on.

Tourism is one of the biggest industries in the U.P. and is becoming bigger and bigger every year. The great thing about living year round in a tourist economy is that you only have to deal with a large population for the peak months of the year. The rest of the time you have vacationland all to yourself. Having been both—first a tourist and now a local—I find myself in a unique position to mediate grievances on both sides. So, I'm about to show you the real power of paper. I've said it before and I'll say it again, I'm here to help.

One thing I've learned from living in the U.P. is that tourists are always asking Yoopers for directions. I've only been here a few years, but I've been asked at least a thousand times how to get somewhere. I can see how this could get annoying.

Yoopers complain that tourists always ask for directions and tourists complain about poor directions from Yoopers. So, I've done the work for everyone. Below is a perforated line. Cut this free prize out and put it in your wallet or purse. If you're a tourist you're all set. If you're a Yooper, hold on to it. Next time a tourist asks you for directions, hand them this:

---

cut here *cut here* *cut here*

HOW TO GET ANYWHERE IN THE U.P. FROM ANYWHERE ELSE

Let's face it, wherever you're from, it's probably south of the U.P. And if you're from Canada or Western Lake Superior, you probably don't need directions because you've been here before. For everyone else, here's how to get to:

St. Ignace: Get to the giant bridge. Drive across it. If the wind doesn't blow you to your death before you reach the other side, congratulations. Your reward is a toll both. Give the person inside twenty percent of your IRA. If you see the tollbooth before the bridge, turn around, you went too far. Go up the hill and hang a right at the exposed rocks. When you smell fish, you're in St. Ignace.

Sault St. Marie: Same directions as St. Ignace but don't turn right at the exposed rocks. Keep going north for about two hours or until your nipples are permanently erect. When you hear more "eh's" than "yes's", you're almost there. Exit for Casino or Wal-mart or exit at the spookiest looking college you've ever seen. If you get pulled over by a cop on horseback, you went too far. Turn around and go back to the Soo, or stay in Soo Canada and frequent one of the many available strip clubs, it's your choice.

Tequomenon Falls: Same as St. Ignace directions, but don't turn right at the exposed rocks. Keep heading north for about forty minutes. When you see absolutely no landmark, head west. Drive through the twilight zone and turn right at the only saloon you've seen all day. Head north until you think the entire earth is nothing but hunting cabins. When you see the sign for Tequomenon, follow their damn directions if you can. Do not get frustrated because there *is* a brewery at the end of all of this.

Naubinway/Manistique: Get a sailboat and put it in the middle of Lake Michigan. Sail due north until you crash into the beach. You are in Naubinway. If you see something that looks like a Dog-man, you are in Manistique.

Whitefish Point: Same as Tequomenon, but don't follow the Tequomenon signs. From Tequomenon, don't forget to turn left, you drunk bastard. Go north until the trees get really short and you need a sweater in July. When you see a giant lighthouse—stop. If you drive into Lake Superior, turn around, you went too far.

Newberry: Go anywhere in Michigan. Commit a felony. You'll get there.

Hiawatha National Forest/Ottawa National Forest: One is on the right and one is on the left. You'll know when you're in and you'll know when you're out. If you're out, go in. If you're in, go out.

Munising/Pictured Rocks: Follow the Hiawatha directions, then head northwest, past the guy who sells animal skins. When you see Hardee's, you're there. To get to the pictured rocks, keep going past Hardee's. Take a left and go past the pasties. Go to the top of the hill, way up there, to the very top. There's a rest area up there. Get out of your car and look out over Lake Superior. Those cliffs out there are the pictured rocks. Figure out how to get out there. If it's wintertime, you may be able to walk.

Marquette: It's the biggest city in the U.P...google it!

Chatham: Munising directions, but bang a left before Hardee's. If you see Hardee's, you went too far, turn around and bang a right, or Marquette directions then southeast. Chatham is southwest of Munising and southeast of Marquette. When you see Munising Ave. or Marquette St. you're not in Munising or Marquette, you're in Chatham, understand?

Escanaba: Follow the Casino signs for the next Chicago concert, or any other popular band whose members are now in their sixties—Joe Cocker, Foreigner, Pat Benatar etc. If you can't find one of these signs you're probably not in the U.P. Go to the U.P. then follow the signs. If you don't know how to get to the U.P, follow directions for Naubinway/Manistique. You'll see a sign.

Menominee: Escanaba directions, then south of Wisconsin. If you can figure that out you're a better person than me.

Houghton/Hancock: If you're going to Houghton/Hancock, you're either coming from Marquette, Sault St. Marie, or anywhere else:

- **From Marquette:** Follow the snowmobiles until you see Michigan tech.
- **From anywhere else:** Go north until you see a sign for a town called Donken. When you stop laughing, you're around Twin Lakes, as opposed to Three Lakes, which you'll pass from Marquette. I'm guessing there's also a Four Lakes and a Five Lakes, maybe even a Six Lakes, but I'm not sure. Right now I'm digging a pond in my back yard. I'm going to name it "One Pond." Anyway, from Twin Lakes keep going north until you see a mall no one shops at. You're in Houghton/Hancock.
- **From Sault St. Marie:** Stand on the lock tower. Jump onto a freighter and head west. When you see a lift bridge with a four-mile long line of cars giving you the finger, you're in Houghton/Hancock.

Copper Harbor: Look at a picture of Lake Superior. Go to the part that appears to have an erection, or Houghton/Hancock directions then north. I mean keep going north until your face is so frozen you look like you're wearing a woman's stocking over your head. If you don't see anything but trees you're going the right way. Keep going north. When all you can do after six billion hours in the car is drink, buy t-shirts, snowmobile or fish, you're there.

Ontonognan: Follow Ottawa National Forest directions. Grab any river. Walk down stream.

Porcupine Mountains: Follow Ontonagon directions, then west and up. I mean way up.

Bruce Crossing, the crossroads of the western U.P: From Lake Gogebic, Bond Falls, Okundekun Falls or Agate Falls, if you see Lake Gogebic, Bond Falls, Okundekun Falls or Agate Falls you've gone too far. Turn around and go back to Bruce Crossing. Or, sober up, you haven't left yet.

Iron Mountain: Escanaba directions then west, not Iron River, Ironwood, Ironheart, Ironbutt, Ironfart or Ironburp.

Ironwood: All the way to the left, after the ice cream eating bears.

Mackinac Island/Straights: All the way to the right, by the ice cream eating people.

Any other place in the U.P. is between two of these points. If you're not sure which ones, it's probably somewhere between Ironwood and Mackinac Island. And remember, "Welcome whomever with whatever, you're welcome to do whichever, wherever and whenever."

---

cut here *cut here* *cut here*

A wise Yooper would run off copies of this, thus saving himself the task of explaining directions for the rest of his life. A wise tourist would run off copies of this for his friends, thus saving them the task of ever asking again.

* *Free Prize in This Book!* first appeared as*: Free Prize in this Column!* in the *U.P. Magazine,* vol. 21 #9, Porcupine Press Publications.

###

COMING SOON!

ALSO

BY

DALE R. HOFFMAN

WEREWOLVES OF NORTH AMERICA

(A FIELD GUIDE)

ABOUT THE AUTHOR

Dale R. Hoffman is a professional comedian and writer. He lives, farms, and hunts with his wife in Michigan's Western U.P. He is available at drumcomic@drumcomic.com

For more information, visit Dale's website at:

http://www.drumcomic.com

CPSIA information can be obtained at www.ICGtesting.com
Printed in the USA
BVOW010935130312

285047BV00001B/23/P

9 780983 512547